The Box Social & Other Stories

The Box Social
AND OTHER STORIES

James Reaney

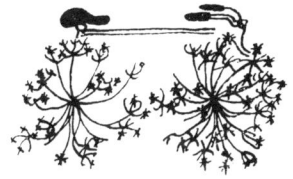

The Porcupine's Quill

CANADIAN CATALOGUING IN PUBLICATION DATA

Reaney, James, 1926–
The box social & other stories

ISBN 0-88984-173-X

I. Title.   II. The box social and other stories.

PS8535.E24B6 1996   C813'.54   C96-930025-5
PR9199.3R43B6 1996

Copyright © James Reaney, 1996.

Published by The Porcupine's Quill, Inc., 68 Main Street, Erin, Ontario NOB 1TO, with financial assistance from The Canada Council and the Ontario Arts Council. The support of the Department of Canadian Heritage through the Book and Periodical Industry Development programme and the Periodical Distribution Assistance Programme is gratefully acknowledged.

This is a work of fiction. Any resemblance of characters to persons, living or dead, is purely co-incidental.

Represented in Canada by the Literary Press Group. Trade orders are available from General Distribution Services.

Copy edited by Doris Cowan.

Cover is after a photograph by the Stratford Beacon Herald. Typeset in Ehrhardt, printed on Zephyr Antique Laid, and bound, at The Porcupine's Quill.

The Library
University of Regina

To Paul Arthur,

bravest of editors
& designer of my first book of poems,
The Red Heart

Contents

The Box Social 9

Fatherhood, Manhood, Circumcision, &c. 13

The Ditch: First Reading 21

Embro 35

Memento Mori 43

The Car 57

The Bully 75

The Ditch: Second Reading 89

Master William Butterfield 97

The Ditch: Third Reading 113

Sleigh without Bells 133

The Box Social

'DO YOU KNOW where I put my gold paint, Auntie?'

She painted some. Swans under bridges with water lilies. Old ladies at windows reading lugubrious Bibles. Tonight she was decorating a shoe box for the box social they were having at the school the next night.

No one expected her to come. She had been quite ill for the last three weeks and hadn't appeared at the last Institute meeting. Now, however, she felt well enough. She was a bit pale and looked much thinner, but she simply had to go. All that evening she sat in the kitchen cutting up old scraps of wallpaper and pasting them on the shoe box, in various patterns, with flour paste. Her box of lunch would be the prettiest there and the men would bid so high for it.

All she needed now was some gold paint, but of course Aunt had gone to bed hours ago.

If Sylvia had any profession at all, it was doing pretty little things like this. Little useless things, for her real vocation had apparently been to stay home and help her aunt with the housework. What she needed now was something to line the box with. It would look so much more beautiful with the sandwiches and the little bottle of olives set against some deep rich colour. Shoe boxes were so wonderfully white.

The rain was falling in soft applause outside.

Her fingers were white from the paste she had been using. The candle in her hand sprouted a yellow willow leaf. She was in the outhouse, searching in the tiny attic for a roll of gorgeous parlour wallpaper she remembered her aunt having left there. Her father always forgot to put down the lids; the two holes stared at her like a man with a large eye and a small one. Finding what she wanted, she stepped out and stood still for a moment. The rain slopped the candle out.

There was the wind in the elderberry bushes; the little things were breathing as hard as if they were swimming across the North Sea; and another sound – that of St. James's bells all the way from town. Some notes were lost, but she gathered it must be twelve. No clock should have any less to say than twelve, unless it were one, at such an hour, so silent and so black.

Twelve black strokes; twelve black hair ribbons.

She walked along the fence beneath the fir trees a bit. The nightshade berries grew here with their wicked fruit. The very next field was lined with furrows, as if it had been a large frown or a copybook. It was not her father's field. Someone else had ploughed it. Furrow after furrow after furrow his house lay away where he now lay sleeping, and she hated him. Then, her own house – a faint pale light from the two kitchen windows. There the decorated shoe box lay almost ready for the box social. Every room of the house, both in their ancient and modern styles, met in parliament on its flat thin sides.

Already the event, the box social, gleamed in the distance like a lantern at the end of a dark stable.

There were half a dozen cars parked at the school. Cars have such beautiful behinds with ruby-red roses that wink at you. Sylvia walked across the fields; neither her aunt nor her father wished to go. She held the precious box in her arms.

It was wrapped in brown paper to protect it from the rain.

Why, you're better!

Yes, I am.

There were thirty people there. No one was as pale as she was. She looked like the queen on the playing card – in her rich red dress, holding the gay box in her lap. All the children's desks were cowering in one corner, for there was to be dancing. Already somebody was sprinkling boracic acid on the floor. Not that it really makes the floor slippery, but everyone is so sure that it does and it feels that much more exciting. The fiddler played six tunes (he only knew five). Mrs Twite wasn't dancing at all, not even with her husband, because they used the school as a Sunday school on Sundays and it would be like dancing in a church. Then, out stole a little green table, and then another green table and another and another; everyone was playing euchre until they should dance again.

I pass, paleface; joker.

They wouldn't be dancing now until after the lunch. Mr Deloney (one of the three farmers in the neighbourhood who owned a silo) was arranging the boxes on the teacher's desk. Sylvia was very careful with her hands lest she eat them. And the teacher had pinned up the winter ornamental border above the west blackboard with all the gay coaches galloping from the north of the room to the south.

This lovely box wrapped in green. What young gentleman wants to eat with a pretty young lady who has wrapped her box in green?

All the men were crowding up.

Hers was almost the last, and he was bidding for it. Five dollars; it had looked so nice. He came straight to her.

'I knew it was yours – recognized the wallpaper. Very pretty. You aren't mad at me any more?'

He sat down, quite comfortable, and began untying the black ribbon. The school clock that they had both looked at together to see if it were recess time ticked loudly above them.

He lifted the lid and sat staring at what lay inside, his great hands unusually white on the top of the green baize card table.

And between them the little shoe box glistened with scarlet wallpaper and gilt like a fairy coffin. Inside it there was the crabbed corpse of a stillborn child wreathed in bloody newspaper.

'I hated you so much,' she said softly.

Fatherhood, Manhood, Circumcision, &c.

ANYWAY, the next thing was that it was a silvery August afternoon, and my mother suddenly calls me into the house from outside, where I had been dressing the dog and the cat in some old-fashioned clothing I'd found in a chest upstairs. Wanting to tell me something important, she sat down in the rocking chair, took me up on her warm, capacious knees.

What she told me was that in a couple of days, nothing to be scared of, there'd be a doctor come out to the farm to perform an operation on me. 'Why?' I asked.

'So you can become a father.'

The member in question looked all right to me, but then I was ill acquainted with it either in health or disease because my parents kept hinting at terrible things that might happen if I had a nice feeling there induced by any touching or exploratory handling. So, other than to hold it for the barest minimum of time to urinate, I just avoided looking down there. Really, I was quite unconscious of a problem, even the pleasurable one. How was I to know where the fathering inability lay?

'They never took us anywhere,' complained a friend of mine lately, 'and they never told you anything. Even in high school they never told you that analytic geometry was algebra and geometry combined. You had to find out everything by yourself. Christ, in South America, the mother goes into the hut with the newlyweds and takes the boy's thing and puts it in for him.'

'Well, my mother practically had to do that,' as I remember other instructive scenes where she quietly took the place of an absent father.

I did everything they told. I was only five.

When I look back, I realize now that for years my mother had been worried about taking this operation step. 'Oh, if only I'd asked the doctor to do it when he was born.'

'Little red boiled-looking thing he was,' said my cousin, a fourteen-year-old girl from the next farm west of us. Following in the footsteps of her Aunt Martha, she was going to be a nurse and so was allowed great latitude in health discussions.

'What difference does it make, at all,' said an uncle's voice, from above the table under which I lay concealed playing with a top. 'Leave the boy be, Lizzie.'

'No, it has to be done before he goes to school. Leave it much later and it'll really hurt like Abraham in the Bible. Agony for days. Could barely walk.'

'Where were you when Jimmie was born,' came relative's voice registering agony at the circumcisive turn the conversation had taken and anxious to change the topic. They were asking this of my father. All were busy making bouquets out of weeds and wild flowers they'd picked up by the roadside on the way back from church. In each bouquet was slowly being formed the first name of someone present, or in the case of a cousin, his fiancée. Back in Ireland, our family had been famous for this.

'What's that humming sound,' asked a deep bass voice. 'Is there a bee under the table, Lizzie?'

'No,' cackled Aunt Alice, notorious for her strange wit, 'it's in the middle of it for you spell "table t-a-BEE-le"!'

After a split second, fists pounded on the table, there were roars of approval, and my mother took the kettle from the coal oil stove out in the woodshed to make tea, and my fourteen-year-old cousin brought some roast beef sandwiches from the pantry, made ready before church, along with a cruet stand.

I had the chance to set the top humming again, but no one appeared to notice it now.

FATHERHOOD, MANHOOD, CIRCUMCISION, &c.

Occasionally, you could hear the crunch of scissors through weed stems, and snipping sounds as string and florist's wire were clipped. Jam jars of water and our three Viennese vases, all with chips and breaks, occasionally tinkled as they were touched.

But I theorized all this; all I could really see were just so many black Sunday shoes, gleaming with polish, sticking through at the bottom of a white linen table cloth that was my private tent.

Suddenly, the bass voice's foot came over and squeezed my mother's left foot; neatly, she kicked him in the right shin.

At last as was his wont, my father replied to the question at the top of this handwritten page: 'Where had he been when I was being born?' I imagined right at my mother's side up in the bedroom over the west room and fighting to be the first to hold me after the midwife and the doctor were through with me.

Not a chance: 'I was suffering pains in that area,' he crept up on his subject. It took me years to understand that, but the *Reader's Digest* finally explained 'couvade' to us all in 1944, or the father suffering birth pangs instead of the mother. Jeremiah in the Bible does have that tremendous passage about such pain as if a man bore his own child. Enough, all this, to frighten the goddess of marriage from the country what with forceps and all those horrors extant in Margaret Mitchell's masterpiece, summed up in two words – 'Butterfly McQueen.'

'Was cultivating down by the marsh hay slough to the east of the orchard. I thought there were enough folks up here. Could tell Jimmie must be born because suddenly there was a lot of white sheets out on the line. It was a warm afternoon, say there came whirlwind out of the slough and it took my cap way up into the air. I looked up for it, and there were white birds floating away up there.'

This silenced everybody for a minute or two. More, I wanted him to say more. But he was so shy and gentle, just the opposite of a Superman. He was an Inframan, yet he'd got through the war. There was the trouble right there, probably. Why, of course, he was a gentleman. That was just beginning to go out of fashion then.

'That's the best tussy mussy between here and Moscow.'

'Why?' came a male voice that had been engaged in argument, low-spoken, with my mother.

'Because I want to be sure he'll be a father.'

'So you're not just doing it because of the Bible.'

'Maybe.'

'You're not – you'll put him off fathering for life, Lizzie, doing it so late.'

'No, now tea.'

'Is it stewed?'

'It is stew-pid,' was the reply, another family ritual that raised huge laughs.

'It wouldn't have hurt at all if the doctor had performed it the moment he was born.'

'What makes you so sure?'

'The baby can't remember anything, so it doesn't hurt.'

Just at this moment, my top stopped spinning and made the most ugly dying sounds, shuddering against the middle legs the table had to support its six boards. As if a theatre curtain the corner of the table cloth was bunched up by a large, hairy-backed hand, and an equally long arm, encased in black, scratchy tweed with a cuff-linked shirtsleeve, came over and fished me out onto a bony big set of knees prickly to sit on because of the indestructible suiting, bought once for a wedding, worn once a week for church, once for that day when its owner opted for underground farming.

'Here we are talking about him. Jimmie, do you understand what we've been saying, my small jug with big ears.'

This was followed by an alarming, whiskery kiss on the nape of my neck.

'Of course, he does not,' said my mother. 'He's too young to take it all in. Look, Haimish. It's for you and there's your name in good Scottish Gaelic upon it.'

On a Queen-Anne's-lace background, my mother had skilfully printed her version of my name in yellow toadflax and blue chicory. She wasn't Irish like all the others at the table; her mother was Highland Scottish, and her father was German. They did everything differently from us.

My father now diffidently unveiled his bouquet. It was much tinier and tighter than mother's — a nosegay for Tom Thumb, a masterpiece. From an armful of Queen-Anne's-lace flowers he had extracted any number of the tiny red male flowers that sit in the very middle of their harem of white florets. These he had attached to an old pin paper to make 'Jimmie' and then let loose with orange hawkweed, also known as devil's paintbrush and false dragonmouth.

I grabbed both the offerings and held them to my nose. I had never seen or smelt anything so beautiful.

'Which one do you like the better?' shot out Aunt Alice who was not above enjoying family quarrels.

'Both,' I replied after a pause. My mother had warned me never to play favourites.

Again, a roar and applause and a falling upon the roast beef sandwiches with a twirling of the cruet stand to get the appropriate condiment — mustard or vinegar, pepper and salt, being highly favoured.

'So he could be a father.' Imagine a mother dealing that particular card so soon. One other thing, another card, came tumbling out. In a month's time, after I'd recovered from the operation, I'd be attending school for the first time. But this school business, eh? — only for a year, and then back home for the rest of my life to finish dressing up the cows, the pigs, and the horses for a circus I was planning with the hired man.

Then, I forgot all about it only to be mystified one evening when my mother, after we had finished washing the dishes, took the dishpan to the stove and filled it with hot water from the tank. She was going to give me a bath up in the room above the summer kitchen where she and I slept.

This was before we had electricity, so it was a shadowy scene with a lamp up there, a naked boy facing a shadowy much taller figure in an apron.

'But, I don't want to be a father,' I said.

Her face went white.

'Why not, Haimish?'

'You remember when I asked you why I have no brothers and sisters, and you said – Father didn't want any? He didn't want me either. And I don't want them.'

'Oh, Haimish, you never said anything for five years, and now you're breaking my heart with such talk. I think I prefer the years of silence. Do what you like then, but at least I'm giving you the choice if you change your mind.'

Thank goodness I restrained myself from saying she could get the doctor to cut out my tongue if it was silence she wanted. So, she kissed me good night, and took the lamp off downstairs. 'No,' she had said, 'the event was not to be tomorrow.' I could hear my father talking down in the kitchen with the threshing man, Mr Schmidt, who'd be bringing over his machine in the morning. Sleep.

In the morning, I was too excited by the threshing preparations to remember yesterday's forebodings. My mother bade me help her chop up cabbages, and we were working away when suddenly, after a glance out the window, she cleared everything off the kitchen table, oil cloth and all, gave the surface of it a wipe, and the verandah door darkened with two doctors in dark business suits, red-haired, father and son. On my mother's side, they were close cousins, and it was to be the son's second operation ever that morning, having just cut off a lump on the back of a nine-month-old baby over several farms. So I learnt later.

All very well, but by that time, I had vanished. I can still feel the difference as my bare feet left the lawn around the house and hit the soft pineapple weed and stinking mayweed of my father's barnyard. In front of all the men waiting for the threshing machine to arrive, each one with a fork, those two red-haired doctors and my mother chased me back into the house yard, but I got down into the cellar and out through the house again back to the barnyard. If I could just make it to the barn, they'd never find me.

Ominously, the neighbours gathered to help my father just stood and watched.

I ran straight at my father who picked me up and held me tight. I began to cry. With delight. It was the first time he had hugged me since I started remembering things and I can feel yet the sheepskin coat he wore and his unshaven face. Yes, even on the hottest days, he wore that coat outside with long woollen underwear under his pants and shirt. He was always cold.

'Jimmie. Let's go on in and show them. What are we afraid of?'

At last, a father was telling me to be one. Small chauvinist that I was, I wanted him to touch me, the leather of the coat – hard, and the wool collar soft and warm. So that was why I had kicked up such a fuss? I wanted him to do something, and he was doing it. It was all right if he entered the kitchen and laid me down on the table, then walked out.

The older one pressed a screened mask against my nose and something went 'whiff whiff'. The young one took down my pants, and the yellow ceiling of the kitchen buzzing with cobwebs, plaster flakes and flies went upside down. Black.

My friend and I discussed this at art school years later.

First of all, he pointed out that I had been a ten-month pregnancy. I was too happy, so the doctors and the midwives had to chase me out of there. Next, early childhood's all very well, but overstay at your peril – Mother got them to chase me out of that with a sharp knife.

The Ditch: First Reading

The Difference between a Mother and a Father

December 31, 1937

Dr Laurence T. Gemmell, Superintendent,
Ontario Hospital for the Insane,
Pottersburg, Ontario (Box 340, London, Ontario)

Dear Sir:

Please find enclosed a copy of an essay one of my students wrote for me at the collegiate here on the topic of 'The Difference between the Mother and the Father in Literature and Life'. I have not typed out the literary part of Robert's essay which used the prose works of James Joyce, some of them smuggled into the country since as you may have heard *Ulysses* is banned in Canada. I hope you are not going to tell the Principal here that I have been corrupting the minds of the local youth. What I have copied out is the boy's account of his own parents – and since you interviewed him directly after his father's death, you will be able to provide valuable background, no doubt to your notes taken at that time. I do query however, just how you are going to handle this material in your forthcoming book on Melancholia and Depression. I don't think that Robert minds, but his permission should it not be asked? The poor father is dead and cannot sue you from the grave, although you should visit the grave in Avondale Cemetery here – it has a very interesting symbol carved upon it – a Pipes of Pan – perhaps you'd like Robert to explain it to you some time. I dare not ask, because, several times I have noticed his voice and eyes breaking and wet with tears whenever the subject of his father comes up. The neighbours might object to your material because biting things are said about their evil; they violated the most fundamental laws of property and privacy of person it would seem to me although now they are being punished by Robert's stepfather who is almost demonic in draining back water onto their land. I gather several of them have sold up and left the neighbourhood. The mother of the lad is an avid reader of everything – so watch out there, and, of course, the stepfather, our City Engineer, is an intellectual with a library. SO, you will have to talk to them.

If there are any gaps or blanks blame it on me – several times when I have been marking essays on my front porch the wind has snatched whole sheaves away from me as if it wanted to know more about the differences between mother and father. Emily Dickinson says that 'the root of the wind is in the sea', and in the case of Robert, it is a reluctant Sun (his father) who could have lifted so many more little mermen from the fertile sea of the mother's womb but his nerve failed him. I, an aging bachelor should talk!

> Sincerely,
> Lloyd Trethewey

The Difference between the Mother and the Father in Life

Dear Mr Trethewey:

I am going to write this essay to you in the form of a letter since that makes the going much easier than formal essay style. I guess many would say that I've already covered the subject and that very vulgarly in my story about circumcision which placed fifth in the *Star Weekly* contest. I know personally readers who vomited after reading the darn thing. Oh well. But, right off the bat I will say this that in our Little Lakes the vulgar farmer way of talking about the difference between man and woman – after all the most obvious difference between a mom and a pop is – tense yourself for ugliness, Mr Trethewey! – 'pricks' and 'cracks.'

In the case of my parents, I used to feel that she was father and mother to me and that he was – a brother to her and an uncle to me, or even a brother, at times younger than I was. There were two years when he was father to me – really a father and thrilling those years were. You need a father to protect you from the mother, and she should shield you from him so you're a constant mix of the two like a painting that's using black and white. There was even a local farmer who lived at some distance from us down in Blanshard, father of one of our teachers here who teaches physical training she learnt in Sweden and Germany with folk dancing and proper preparations for the parallel bars, the horse etc., preparations sadly lacking in the male department at our collegiate. I think our Phys-Ed teacher was trained at one of those concentration camps they say they're setting up in Deutschland, *nicht wahr?* I digress, but you do have a difference between mom and pop right there: educated mother, usually a former school teacher, husband – an oaf with no high school at all except the Orange Lodge. To get back to the lady whose father was a farmer in Blanshard – you can't mark me 'digression' because people are allowed to digress in letters, aren't they? Well, anyway, this farmer had once been a professor at the University of Toronto and had been fired for writing an indiscreet letter to the *Globe* about hiring the Chancellor's son-in-law at a higher salary than anyone else was getting. He used to go around to schools and churches lecturing on mental and health problems from the viewpoint of Christian humanism (what would that be, I wonder). Young people don't want to know about that, they want to know about – there should be a book to tell you if you're in love or not and is there anything wrong about being really crazy about someone of your own sex and – some drawings showing the sex act with a woman would come in happily. What did Oscar Wilde do, that sort of thing. But, I do remember one thing from the lecture and that was that the woman was religion and the man was reason. In the case of my mother and father, she was both – she had to be, and he was religion – inner, intense, depressed, and melancholic.

He never touched me much; she was always patting and sculpturing me. Fathers in our district are not noted for public affectionate displays; it was five years ago that I saw a man embrace another man as they parted forever. No, whippings with razor strops were the father's way of touching his sons in our Little Lakes district, usually the old man's pants falling down if he used his belt. I did know one father though – Nig Hoffmeyer – who gave his son a bottle of potato wine to take to school with him for his lunch-time beverage. My father didn't whip me – although I can remember I must have stirred his temper dreadfully by something I did at table aged four, for I suddenly found myself not at the dinner table (noon) but running down the back lane hoping he was not after me. I don't think I came back to the house till the moon was just coming up and I can remember mounting the back steps to the bed where I slept with my mother in the moonlight.

Odd, but I had no idea at the time that it was odd that they didn't sleep together. What I did notice was that I had no brothers and sisters so I asked mother where they were and if any might be forthcoming. She said that my father didn't want to have any.

Apparently, when I was born he was thrown for a loop by

the fact that he would now have to support me, that marriage was more complicated than he had thought and he wanted to load mother and me up in the waggon or maybe the car, if it were going, and take us over to her father's place for good. This led to a visit from my grandfather who persuaded him not to do this and also promised him any dead wood he found in his bush – we had no woodlot – if he ran into problems with fuel for the stoves. At this time, my father was running the farm on shares with a former hired man and lying down in the kitchen on the couch a lot, unable to move for just feeling – sad.

For one dollar and five minutes of his time, Dr Fraser diagnosed 'melancholia' – I have the bill and diagnosis framed up over my desk. Dearly would I love to know what goes on in that spooky old house of his on Waterloo and Downie – have you read *King's Row*, Mr Trethewey?

Oh God, I can remember when very young when it still seemed their marriage was one – they would clean out the stable together after milking and I would help them, dipping my toy shovel into the gutter, loving the smell, proud of us all mucking about and their praise at my 'skill'. I loved the barn then and the animals. But, slowly all this withered somewhat because he really hadn't wanted to be a farmer, it came out, and he really didn't seem to care what I became. Well, he did care. When I started to school I had my first book – a reader costing seven and a half cents from Eaton's with absolutely riveting stories in it such as the Little Red Hen both in handwriting and print. I am hell on books, reading them to pieces and leaving them outside where he found my first reader slipped down in the woodpile all wet, red washed out to pink, covered with slug slime and bark dust. So he got me a fresh copy which I still possess. In the back, I've drawn something I call the Alphabet River with all the letters flowing into it and it eventually coming to an unnamed sea. I can remember the feel of the wool on the collar of his sheepskin coat where my face pressed because he was holding me up in the yard somewhere to see something. I can also remember him at the fair taking me for a ride on the merry-go-round and standing beside me so I wouldn't fall off. Later, he held me near an airplane whose propeller, before he could stop me, I started to turn by reaching over his shoulder. There was a rush of people to interrupt this as the engine coughed a bit as if appreciative of my interest.

My father never swore – he was gentle, he worshipped Lord Alfred Tennyson, he has written in the back of his Bible ten ways to know if you're saved. Someone once saw him, looking back to see why his waggon was so slow, wrestling with a fellow in the ditch, but he never taught me to wrestle nor did he teach me to ride although he'd done that for his bread during the war as a messenger, and when we would suddenly descend on him asking for help – making a window-stick for the School Fair in 1934, he would say as he measured a plank and told me where to cut – 'Don't you know how to do this?' 'No, dad. Where would I learn? I'm only seven years old. Do you think I sneaked around places before I landed here.' 'Yes,' he smiled. 'Your mother found you at the bottom of the garden under a cabbage so she says. How do I know where you were before that?'

That was another thing. I couldn't get any more satisfactory thing out of him about my origins than that, and, as I put two and two together, I realize now I've been too hard on him. He was not well, and I've had a touch of it too and it's melancholia freezing your guts with constipation and just making you so still. So you think, 'Farm after farm is afflicted with spinsters and bachelors – there's a seven bachelor farm near Port Stanley – men and women who never married. The damn Presbyterian church despite all the good work of Burns has frozen their reins with fear.' They need a big statue of

THE DITCH: FIRST READING

Priapus up on the clock shelf instead of that damn Massachusetts clock would put you off your stroke – the result of reading your copy of *Ulysses*, Mr Trethewey, but – then why have I the right to talk? Unlike the precocious Jim Joyce so blessed in living in a place filled with loose women, I'm eighteen and still not a father, thanks Mom, and still a virgin – where are the prostitutes in this town, there used to be a brothel, where has it gone to? All the girls – save a mythical one or two – are tighter than barn doors *und so weiter*. All these old maids and bachelors are, I note, Scots or Scots Irish. The Irish Catholics breed more and the Germans have taken over the township. They don't hold back, and therein lies the difference between my two parents because my mother was only half Presbyterian; my grandmother was German, and *they* have no old maids and no bachelors. They love eating and kissing and hugging and, I gather, bed activities. I can tell because when I slept with my mother she would hold me in her arms all night. You could feel electricity flowing out of her through you. But father was frightened of the mating act and cold and – not in love with himself though. He feared his sex which had got him into trouble when he was little and caused terrible scenes of attempted cutting throat and other places so I'm told now by aunts who always seem to enjoy telling me and my mother more and more stories of just what a madhouse his boyhood was. *It* does get you into trouble – how do you expect us kids at school to learn all those dreary irregular verbs with a fire cracker tied to us slowly smouldering away all day and all night.

But the difference between the two came out dramatically in a scene I witnessed at a threshing when I was about eight and to tell you about it I have to paint in Victor McKersie, our hired man.

His night off was Saturday and after he had changed into a good suit and lathered his hair with Booster shampoo, which had the most enchanting witch hazel smell and all his chin was barbered over twice, looking really smart, he'd throw me up in the air, catch me and ask as he waved me around himself, his hands on my crotch and my neck, what I wanted him to bring me from town. My wants were simple – a certain kind of jelly bean in a white bag selling at a penny which I gave him; but he often came back without jelly beans but other things; for example, a set of sand pile toys, seaside crayfish and starfish made out of coloured tin that you could do *bas reliefs* with in wet beaches, or a Japanese salt and pepper set – yellow salt shaker with a round head, brown pepper shaker with square head, a cork in the bottom that usually got pushed into the shaker and had to be fiddled out with a needle. There seemed to be no explanation of who really chose these things or if he won them at the fair or was advised about them by some lady friend of the night or?

Victor's most important gift to me was a pressed glass candy container in the form of a miniature railway signal lantern whose green glass chimney glass was filled with small round candies – bright pastels shimmering through frosted green glass. I loved it the moment he gave it to me on a Sunday morning, felt it in my pocket all through Sunday school, have more or less centred my life around it. I love it. It's beautiful. I've never opened it to eat the candies. I just have to think of it and I go wild and soft and effervescent inside and seem in a different state and then I get exhausted thinking about its beauty and have to lie down and rest. Is that what love of a woman is, is supposed to be like? I've still got it in a small box where I keep such ravishing keepsakes. People say – my Uncle Headrick told my mother that she shouldn't try to write her autobiography from her birth but from when she was reborn in Christ Jesus. I've never felt as intensely about Him as I have about the miniature green lantern. But I don't need to look at it any more.

THE DITCH: FIRST READING

It has turned out to be just enough that I know it's there inside the Dutch biscuit box (Frou Frou) from my stepgrandmother's store she used to keep over in Guelph. There are two other things that rate in this account of things people gave me that changed me. My father, taking note of Victor getting me away from him and becoming my 'real' father, one noontime in summer came back from town with a new scythe blade he needed and – a Pan pipe of pressed green and marbled pink, black Bakelite. I was rocking in the rocking chair quite wildly, thinking and humming to myself and sometimes singing, by request, songs to my mother busy getting the dinner ready, and then he came in with this. It was like putting an oriole in your mouth, and sliding it up and down to bigger birds and then smaller birds at the top. And it tasted – that celluloid taste that is involved with the way Kewpie dolls attract me. The third thing was from my mother – she let me have an envelope that had a gold and bronze and silver and shiny gold lining of texture paper. I used to close that and open it by the hour at the kitchen table with the wind roaring around outside and the fire just leaping about in the stove fighting the early spring cold with warmth, warmth. Then, I'd shut my eyes and put my hand inside the envelope to feel the gold and the bronze. I'll tell you about my four favourite flowers and fruit experiences later, but of course there was one other quite other kind of thing that haunted my childhood and that was going suddenly upstairs to my mother's room to get the belt for my brown velvet short Goosey Gander pants – we were going off to grandfather's in the buggy. She'd taken a sponge bath with the bowl and jug up on the dresser and was just drying herself when I ran in and happened to glance at her – that is, the black triangle of hair at the pediment of her legs, then I glanced away and got the belt and ran downstairs.

'You shouldn't be looking,' she said after me.

'It's too late now,' I murmured. 'I'll pretend I didn't,' because it was a big turning point to see that.

Sacred black triangle where once I came forth, a red little boiled-looking thing into this world of blacks and whites and seas and suns and clouds and smacks for being naughty and caresses for being good and – the sound of 'and' itself?!!!!! AND! Ampersand – & – is a good symbol for marriage, eh?

Looking at my father one day when he was taking a public bath in our big tin bathing tub, specially made by our local whitesmith or tinsmith, Mr Rosier, I observed with shock that he had teats on his chest – to nurse what or whom?

Like a clap of thunder it came to me that men and women weren't so different as I'd thought – Nature cheated and using the same model did a dangle or an inner sinus for it to penetrate, but when it came to the chest just admitted defeat. At the time, I can remember a positive storm of bitterness seething over me: first there was no Santa Claus, then no Easter Bunny, now no real gap between Man and Woman – we were all women. Ugh! No, I wanted –? I'm sure if you investigate the belly of a bull you *don't* find a vestigial udder!

My mother, confiding in me once, said she thought of going to the orphanage and bringing home a little girl and a little boy for me to play with. My heart leapt up although since then having actually been in the orphanage for an experimental stay when I really fell out with my stepfather once, I shudder at the possibilities of getting a lunatic or a barn-burner or, worst of all, Mr Trethewey, a bore. Better, my dear mother, to find some little babies exposed to die in the ditch or on the church steps – except you don't know what the parents were like, do you?

Our story began to really darken when one day we learnt that my 'real' father, our hired man, Victor McKersie, would have to leave us. The events behind this were as follows: our neighbours had turned against us – first they insulted my mother by spreading lies about her behaviour to my father, and that within my hearing at a threshing at Ally Porte's. Next, they started moving the fences in and draining their water onto our farm, unfortunately in a valley between their farms on higher lands.

Victor McKersie, who cannot read or write, and so has some pretty wild ideas at times, he took a rifle and went over to one of our enemies and threatened to shoot him if he didn't stop the slander and the water. Then, he went to another neighbour and said he would burn his barn down if he didn't treat us better.

The sheriff of the whole county came out and told Victor to get out of the county in three days or else it'd be the worse for him.

I cried at losing him, and then he did an amazing thing, he said for me to pack my duds and run away with him. He had relatives way up in the Bruce, he even had an old stone-strewn farm which'd still be good for sheep, and we could live there, and he'd bring me up. There was even a girl who had been waiting since before he went off to the war and met my father who still said she was waiting for him. He mentioned her because I had said I didn't feel like just being with a father, I wanted some sort of mother. This ended up with my writing a letter for him saying that he wanted to marry her but was too shy to speak, and too illiterate to write. Then, he simply picked me up in one hand, with his waggon and trunk pulled along by the other, and so kidnapped me.

My parents gave chase in the buggy and tracked us down about Gadshill which is a little three foot rise in the centre of the Ellice swamp north of here.

I was crying because I was afraid, but also more deeply, because he was the man who had brought me the green lantern filled with pastel candies. I loved him. He loved me; ever since he came to the farm. I was the child he had watched over and played with and given Japanese salt and pepper shakers to.

My parents got him a ticket at Gadshill Junction for a train to Kincardine so he wouldn't have to pull his trunk in his waggon all the way, and when they said goodbye, he and my father embraced – not a thing men do around here unless they've been through Hell together as those two had during the war.

Now came a nice time with my dad. He didn't seem to have so many attacks, and he ran the farm himself, and he decided to fight back at the neighbours by digging a ditch to drain the water to the south end of the farm and so into the Harmony municipal drain. In the middle of a big ironing session with my mother, he came in and swept me away to helping him. He rescued me from the girl's work I was rapidly becoming addicted to. I love baking bread.

Is that the difference between a mother and a father, Mr Trethewey? What did you want to know for anyhow, you old Peeping Tom with no chick nor child to your name, you batten on our problems, and yet – I know you love us, and we love you, because you're the only one to ever ask us about our feelings.

I've asked my schoolmates about what they think, and a lot of them say – they're writing down how they are far more afraid of their fathers than their mothers. I think their dads resent them taking up so much of the mother's time.

Mother would never dig a ditch. Father can't iron. Maybe I'm going to be both a father and a mother since I can do both?

Mr Trethewey, isn't it explained – my topic – that we live on a great big round thing, an electric battery flying through the stars, or whirled around a merry-go-round to a star that is whirled around some invisible otherness, God as a little boy playing with his whirligig rope or bolo, that Argentinian leather thong, they use it to catch ostriches with on the ostrich farms, tangles up their legs, wraps itself around them, saw them in the *National Geographic* – isn't that this huge battery has a negative and a positive magnetic pole – and our father lies with this pole sticking up from his midriff somewhere in icy Baffin Land while our mother with the same pole negatively sinused deep into her bowels, like the inside of a lined, with velvet – no gold paper, tubular envelope (French letter!) – Mother near Mount Erebus in Antarctica.

Oh, one day Antarctica and Arctica (black she-bear of the legend, white Zeus of the myth), be one!

>Your attentive
>and affectionate red-boiled student,
>Robert

Embro

I AM A SCHOOLMASTER, and in the autumn of 1875, I took a position as the teacher in Embro, quiet enough village until the accident, situated on the slope of land that comes down through the township of Zorra and so to the banks of the Thames River.

My landlady, a big little widow named Mrs Gracey, also swept out the school at a penny a time, and, living with her as I did in her cottage on the edge of a field known as Mother Brown's Hill, why I soon learnt a great deal about the village and its surrounding farms.

For example, I learnt that the hill was named after her sister, long dead and regarded locally as having some mystery about her death.

I also learnt that her hill was a wonderful hill to sleigh down, a fact I liked since I had brought my toboggan, named *Snowflake*, with me. I learnt too that I must never go sleighing there on Sunday, must avoid the deserted barnyard in the hollow of the hill, and, above all, never drink from the well in that barnyard.

Yes, it was a marvellous hill to sleigh on, and one bright frosty afternoon five children and myself went all the way to the top of Mother Brown's Hill, then down! Down all the way almost to the river, farther than any other sleigh or toboggan!

I was telling Mrs Gracey of this feat as we walked home from the school in the December twilight. I remember she seemed to be listening until something in a certain store window caused her to turn away from me and interrupt me with:

'Look what that fat young villain has put in his window! Oh, is that where they were all these years!'

In a corner of the window, the storekeeper, a young fellow with flaxen hair and not a line in his face, was even now placing some dolls carved out of wood. They were character dolls – school children dressed as living thirty years back; next he placed a taller doll which I blushed to recognize as a 'schoolmaster' doll not unlike myself. Teachers, however, no longer wear long black coats and, as this one did, carry a switch.

Last of all, the blond storekeeper placed in a position of honour quite a different kind of doll – a factory-made china doll with a pink dress and hair even paler than his own.

'That's an old doll of his mother's,' whispered Mrs Gracey. 'He'll be selling her old hats next. Sir, you go in ask him how much he wants for those other dolls and I'll go home get your supper. I'd go in myself, but I'd just lose my temper at him and hit him one – in you go now!'

With this, she walked off. Reluctantly, I went into the store and asked the man about the price of the dolls. There were other people in the store and I could hear them laughing. They laughed some more when he replied that I could have the pretty doll, but the character dolls were being saved for a wealthier collector.

'Found them all in a trunk my mother must have put up in the attic,' added the storekeeper. 'Shall I wrap up your dolly for you, schoolmaster?'

Quite embarrassed, I stumbled out of the store and made my confused way to the edge of the village where the white expanse of Mother Brown's Hill stretched out above me like the wing of a giant seabird.

The lamps were coming on in house after house; in Mrs Gracey's cottage a dimmer light showed – a candle – and by its light I was soon eating fried potatoes and salt pork with boiled kale as I told her what had happened. Mrs Gracey's reply was:

'No good will come of Gurney putting those dolls in the

window like that. Something dreadful will come of it, mark my words, sir.'

Naturally, I asked 'Why?' and this is the story my landlady told me. It's the kind of story that cries out to be drawn on fresh, white snow with an icicle. Listen! Look!

When Mrs Gracey was a very small girl, she had an older sister named Ann. The family's name was Brown. The Browns farmed the land containing the sleighing hill and lived in the house and used the barn now all in ruins that stood in the hollow of that hill. When Mrs Gracey's older sister asked her parents for a doll, her father, who did not believe in store-bought things, carved some dolls for her, very amusing ones which her mother then dressed. There was a rumour that occasionally the dolls could be heard talking to each other; be that as it may, Ann took the dolls for a sleigh ride one day on a small hand sleigh her father had also made for her. I enquired after this sleigh's name. Mrs Gracey thought a bit, then said *Bluebird*.

Also taking her dolls for a sleigh ride that day was the storekeeper's mother. Millie was her name, and, as you have seen, her doll was a very handsome, flashy specimen.

Now, just how it started, no one could quite tell, but the two girls fell to blows about the dolls. Millie said her doll was far prettier than those ugly wood-and-horsehair ones of Ann's. Ann was about to fight this when her mother called her into the barn to help wash some milk pails.

When she came back, Millie and all the dolls were gone, but written in the snow was the following message:

'I have thrown your ugly dolls down that well you have and I have gone home with Barbara, the prettiest doll in all the world. Millie.'

Ann screamed, sleighed over to the well and fell in. Her body was never recovered. 'And so Millie lied,' said Mrs Gracey as the clock struck ten and the candle we'd had our supper by had long ago suffered replacement. 'She hadn't really thrown the dolls in the well; no, she'd hidden them up in the attic of that store and now her son, long after she's dead, puts them up for sale in his window.'

'But, Mrs Gracey, didn't I see Ann's gravestone in the churchyard?'

'Yes, but she's not there. You may have noticed that there was no death date. Mark my words, now that it's known where the dolls really are she'll come back from the well in whatever strange country she stays in down there and get them back.'

At this, Mrs Gracey stood up. The candle cast a huge shadow of her on the ceiling.

'Or,' she added, 'my sister will see that those dolls are brought to her. Oh – she's waited too long!'

The next day, it being a Saturday and the snow crisp and slippery, like a fool I put the whole absurd story out of my head and started to sleigh down the hill with children and young people doing likewise all around me. I remember now that I heard the church bells ring for five o'clock. Suddenly, in the white blur beside me I observed that a sleigh called *Thistle* bearing four or five of my scholars was being swept as if by a mysterious tide over into the hollow where the ruined farm buildings were. But so was my *Snowflake*, steer her as I might. Only with a mighty effort did I pull clear of the outlying walls and orchards of the Brown homestead and make it safely down the rest of the hill. I looked back to see the sleigh of my five students slide around all sorts of obstacles and disappear into the well with a great splash.

Before I ate supper, and a late, late supper it was too, the usual scenes at such disasters took place. The parents came and wept – grappling hooks were lowered to no avail, crowds gathered, went away, then came back again. There were still frantic fathers and mothers there when I finally gave up trying to dive down to the bottom of the well, for in summer my pastime is swimming and I have won many prizes for diving and long-distance swims. Huddled in a blanket, I made it home to my landlady's where a hot fire and a glass of whisky awaited me.

'Sir, do you feel up to trying it again?' she asked, stirring some hot gruel she was preparing for me.

'Sure, but first I'll have to die of the shivers.' There was an ominous pause, then she raised her apron and revealed the six character dolls I had first seen in the store window tied on a string around her waist.

'Mrs Gracey, how did you get those dolls?'

'Never mind!' An hour later, I was on my sleigh at the top of Mother Brown's Hill. Given a farewell push by Mrs Gracey, I slid down waiting in terror for the magnetic pull from the well. It came and slowly, surely I saw the well coming towards me. Someone was watching by it – oh yes, they had placed planks over the well, but as I came up these latter flew up in the air and, with a scream, the watcher fled away shouting that there was a goblin at the well!

When I woke up, I was lying on the other side of a river and all about me was the greenest of grass with not far away a farmhouse with oddly low windows matched by an extremely low door. As oddly, I found myself reckoning that the door was probably as high as Ann had been when she dived into the well after her dolls.

I stooped down and looked in at the tiny paned windows. Inside I could see a kitchen not unlike my landlady's. There was a fire on with a big woman sitting spinning by it. On the table beside her were six dolls – effigies of myself and the children who had disappeared down the well that afternoon above.

I crept over and knocked on the low door.

'Who is it?' came a suspicious gruff voice. 'Is it Millie

come at last to say she's sorry making me fall down a well looking for my bairns that were not hidden there, oh no, but hidden up in the attic of that store, well I'll show you. If I cannot have my dolls back I'll steal real children and a real schoolmaster down that well and I shall keep them here till I get my own back!'

'Ann Brown,' I said. 'I am a pedlar passing along this way and I'd like to exchange some dolls I have in my pack for those dolls I see you have on your table.'

The door flew open.

'Ann Brown, I'd much rather – why don't you come out on your doorstep and see my wares?'

Just then, it began to rain so hard I had to stoop down and enter her house.

'Set my dolls down,' she ordered.

I countered by asking that she first put the dolls on the table in my hands. Very reluctantly she did so. The moment we made the exchange, the dolls on the table changed into real children and I felt a jolt as for a few minutes only there were two of me in the room.

'Oh my dear little ones,' she crooned cradling her long-lost dolls. 'You're home with your mother at last.'

'Now,' said I, 'I wonder if you could tell us how we're to get back to the village?'

'Just walk out the door,' said our hostess, 'and across the big river down there.'

As she spoke, I could hear far away church bells ringing in our village, ringing one of the longer hours. But the children noticed their sleigh hanging up on the wall, along with many others, and insisted on taking it down so that by the time we were ready to go, the door had shut and could not be opened. Then I remember what Mrs Gracey had whispered to me as she gave my toboggan a shove: 'Sir, always remember that down there I've heard it's easy to enter a house, but hard to get out – except when the church bells ring here and then their locks have no power.'

The second time the door opened, Ann distracted the children's attention with a pretty iced cake she brought out from her pantry. She seemed to be waiting for something – perhaps if we didn't get away before dark, we would have to stay ... Forever.

Then, just as twilight was beginning to fall outside, I noticed a look cross her face that meant she heard the bells ringing again. And this look did not go away because up in the village her sister had been clever enough to get the villagers to take turns ringing the church bells all the time, day and night.

I pushed open the door, my other hand holding my toboggan. The scholars ran by me with their sleigh and with a yell she chased after us.

Jumping into the river, we floated across on our sleighs – in my case on my toboggan which I had always called the canoe of the snowdrifts without quite realizing how true that might be.

When we looked back, the whole bank of the river was on fire with her reaching across at us in a giant smoke shape taller than the trees.

But on the other side of a river, we saw a crowd of people looking at us. It was the whole village come to watch the field of dry grass which had caught fire and the bells were ringing to bring helpers to put out the fire before it spread.

It was summer, had been hot and dry for a whole month. We had been away for just under six months.

Well, when we climbed upon the shore, the fire went out and the grass that had apparently been burning appeared quite green again and unburnt.

I and Mr Gracey are the only ones who, when the smoke drifted away, are absolutely sure they saw a little girl run back on the other side of the river and disappear into Mother Brown's Hill.

You can imagine the questions everyone asked. And parents were overjoyed to see their offspring again, but not overjoyed at my neglect of duties in staying underground for six months! For this, they docked my pay, allowing though that I might continue as schoolmaster but no raise just yet. With all that bell ringing, I think their tempers were frayed.

By mistake, this evening, Mrs Gracey and I walked by Gurney's store for the first time since we saw him placing the dolls in his window, still splintered and broken though neatly cobbled back together with long pieces of duck tape.

'Barbara's still there,' I whispered, seeing if I could get a rise out of Mrs Gracey.

'Who's Barbara?' asked Mrs Gracey.

'Millie's doll. Still in the broken window of the store over there. Looking a bit the worse for wear too what with the window not being replaced yet.' A grim silence.

'Don't you think she must be rather lonely without her old friends?'

'Very,' came the reply from my landlady who looked straight ahead.

Memento Mori

Loyal O'Hanley
Lot 39
Concession XII
West Williams
Middlesex County
Ontario
Canada
The New World
The British Empire
The Earth
The Milky Way
The Stars

AS A BOY, Loyal O'Hanley inscribed this stairway to the stars on the flyleaf of every book in his small but largely curious library, annexed from books already in various places around his parents' farmhouse: Rider Haggard's first novel, *Dawn*, which has a remarkable scene where a wicked lady called Lady Bellamy says as she very dramatically poisons herself: 'Ah, stars who look down on me and this poor clown. Evil Winking Algol, clearest Aldebaran, and blood red Antares in Scorpio, in a moment I shall find myself in your depths or in the mind behind you or far beyond.' At this point, Lady Bellamy poured the vial of deadly poison into the wine which boils up furiously.

I think that Loyal often thought of what Lady Bellamy said about being 'in their depths or in the mind behind you or far beyond'. To the stars and beyond them if at all possible became his quest. There was also in his library a copy of

Maria Monk, a lurid Gothic novel not calculated to push its readers to the stars, but indeed in the opposite direction: cheek by jowl came the most innocuous book ever written. A *Robert Martin's Lesson*, in the Pansy Book Series followed by *Emily of New Moon, Wuthering Heights*, a directory to the County of Armagh, and a Masonic Bible, *Tanglewood Tales, Daniel and the Book of Revelation*, in which Napoleon was Antichrist, so that we're already a century and a bit into the millennium with Christ come back in secret, Webster's *International Dictionary*, Third Edition (Loyal's mother had been a school teacher), *Uncle Tom's Cabin*, and *Christ or Satan*, a religious novel set in modern times (1906) emanating from Tennessee, with demons under beds and looking in the windows of quite ordinary-looking houses with gables just like the O'Hanley house. Particularly striking was the scene where Christ having returned to Earth, New York and the Woolworth Building were seen going up in flames. Since there was no public library at Bornish, aside from Christmas boxes, for his parents encouraged Loyal's reading bent, is it any wonder that reading and re-reading the above, the boy's mind began to take on unusual capacity for seeing odd angles and dark corners. Incidentally, his parents did not know about *Maria Monk* which was hidden under a loose floorboard in their son's bedroom. It was a long time before its occasional reader puzzled out just what the 'criminal connections' actually meant in real life. Real life! What was that? No, the the real life for Loyal was not in the world of things, although he, with book in hand or pocket, managed to help his father on the farm quite well enough; no, the real life was in the kingdom of shadows in the small, much thumbed library, and in the mushroom-and-Indian pipes mental landscape that found its nourishment in the chlorophyll of writers, most of them long since dead.

Therefore, it was quite natural that from a very early age,

Loyal had encouraged himself to believe that he was a changeling, his mother not his mother, his father not his real father. Who his real parents were he never quite dared to say, but in his dreams, at the end of a long avenue of ancient crooked trees, there dangled a tarnished crown. Then too, although the farmhouse where he had been born had the thinnest of walls and the shallowest of attics, he flattered it with the possession of secret passage-ways and hidden dungeons. For hours, he would linger in the pantry imagining that on the other side of the cups and dishes (even though he knew there was a verandah) – imagining that there was a windowless room littered with old books, a guttering candle, and a twin to himself, reading away.

Ordered to clean up the woodshed as his Saturday morning task, an act long overdue, Loyal stood staring at the reflections in a rain barrel half filled with rain and dead leaves. There was an empty turpentine bottle which he picked up and stared at the sun through.

Wheelbarrows of muck and trash and debris did he cart out of that woodshed, long ago a summer kitchen as well as wash house. When it occurred to him that his father had once told him that somewhere as a boy he remembered running across a gravestone in the woodshed, Loyal began to disturb the rubbish more thoroughly although he still had not come anywhere near exposing the floor of the place, said to be of rough cobble stones.

Loyal paused, set down his shovel, and let the vision of the brown muck which was neither sawdust nor earth sink into his soul; it was a way he had of dowsing for things, ideas as well, hidden secrets. Other interesting things he might run across were: the finger of a hired man accidentally chopped off – which the madcap fool had then tried to put down Loyal's neck while Mr O'Hanley was applying a tourniquet and Mrs O'Hanley was phoning the doctor. Often enough to delay things, pieces of old newspaper appeared – Amelia Earhart, the Cleveland torso murderer, a complete page of the comic strip *The Katzenjammer Kids* still with the two panels of Mr Dingelhoofer above. Loyal wept at the colours – mysteriously magic because they were made of scores of tiny coloured dots.

Well, he did not finish cleaning the woodshed that day, but on his fourteenth birthday, when he had for some months reluctantly said farewell to an excellent soprano voice, much appreciated at St. Joseph's Church, he did, still not quite finishing the Herculean cleansing of a place far worse than the Augean stables, well – he, his shovel sudden hit the marble of a stunningly gleaming, white, much carved gravestone. Pulling it free after much digging and pulling and prying, Loyal's breathing quickened as he managed to read through the dirt – some very strange carving underneath which appeared:

Souviens Gabrielle Volets
Mort August 7, 1900

For a long while, no one knew that he had found it, so carefully did he hide it, but they did notice a change in his behaviour as if more than just the loss of a treble voice was bothering him; there was the look of an obsession with some secret, dangerous joy, a joy that marble is clever at feeding particularly if it is the Venus de Milo with her full milkful breasts, seen in a picture book in his music teacher's hallway waiting room, or even more tellingly the torso of a god, male, headless, legless, armless, a broken off stump in the secret place of virility.

Discreetly, Loyal winkled out of his father and mother all that they knew about his new companion. To begin with, his mother had never seen it, but she remembered her husband's relatives saying things about it that he himself had forgotten. For example, the gravestone had been made for someone else, and then hastily adapted to quite a different kind of person, e.g., much younger and – *not* Protestant. Since Mrs O'Hanley was, unlike her husband and son, a Protestant, this information had lasted with her. It was from her parents' house that most of the books such as *Christ or Satan* emanated.

Mr O'Hanley said after thinking about it for a while that no, Loyal's thought that somebody must have been buried in the woodshed was not so, but that what had properly happened – probably – was that when St. Anthony's Chapel with its cemetery was finally abandoned and deconsecrated, in the process of moving the gravestones, the coffins, and the church furniture too sacred to be deserted, this gravestone had been taken into the empty church and left behind. Loyal pricked up his ears at this; that meant the corpse would have been taken to the cemetery at St. Joseph's in Bornish and placed in an unmarked grave. Part of his obsession was to find out what Gabrielle Volets had looked like, for his grandfather had said that she was Father Volets's youngest sister, with some mystery about her – thrilling insanity? Really the priest's by-blow, a changeling left at his doorstep? His housekeeper's niece? A hundred years ago, the bishop of the diocese in which St. Joseph's and St. Anthony's lay had been Canadien and had encouraged priests of his ilk; fifty years ago, after his spectacular lapse into insanity upon incurring great debts for the diocese, he had been replaced by an Irishman who had transferred Father Volets to Paincourt, fifty miles south of Bornish or so, maybe more like eighty, and after a period of fifteen years when St. Anthony's Chapel lost most of its congregation, uprooted it and actually sold the wooden building to old Mr O'Hanley for use as a pig house! Yes, there it sat, white with green trim, pointed coloured glass windows, far more filled with pigs than it had ever been filled with human worshippers, just occasionally to Loyal's humorous eye sometimes becoming a pig church, a porcine prayer house, with whole rows of eager worshipers at the trough, superintended by Loyal as deacon: 'Ite, missa est,' he would shout at the oinking congregation and although they would not 'Ita,' nevertheless they did look up at him.

About this time, Loyal had an excellent English and history teacher, Mr Kearns at the high school and it was he who suggested that the next time he went to London, he would enquire at the diocesan chancery if there had been a priest at St. Anthony's after Father Volets. Yes, there had – a Father Flaherty.

The Flaherty family still existed in Ellice Township, fifty miles away, and, after some correspondence, Loyal bicycled all the way to their farm where an ancient hired hand told him that yes, in order to keep St. Anthony's Chapel open, for it still at that time was used for weddings and funerals, even christenings, Father Flaherty would get him to drive over in the buggy with a broom and some dusters, and when they got there, opening the chapel with a large iron key, he would bid the hired man sweep out the church – dead leaves, the occasional dead butterfly – and then perhaps, with only the hired man as communicant, say mass. 'He was a great one for saying masses, was Father Flaherty,' said Loyal's informant rocking back and forth in his rocking chair and re-lighting his pipe, 'Why every morning he'd go out to the mailbox there and there'd be ten letters with ten dollars each in them asking him to say a mass for the good of someone's soul in his previous parishes. He had bagfuls of ten-dollar bills until, at last, the diocese forced him to cough up forty thousand dollars.'

Well, at last the bishop decided to – deconsecrate.

'Oh, yes, I do remember that gravestone – it was tipped up against the door for a door stop. Not at all like a Catholic stone with a cross, a sponge, a spear, five nails, that sort of thing we have around here, but a woman getting her hair cropped by an angel? A skull and crossbones, pyramids, and Lord knows what it all had on it.'

And so when the chapel became a pig stable on the O'Hanley farm, the gravestone must have been thrown into the woodshed and perhaps used as a cutting table for meat during butchering time because there were great disfiguring gashes on the obverse side.

At first, Loyal thought to approach his spiritual guardian and offer to put the gravestone back where it belonged. That would entail the thrilling possibility of finding out from the burial register where Gabrielle had been reburied. The sexton had a long stick with which he tested the ground for occupants below – always reminding Loyal of his mother testing the doneness of a cake in the oven with a straw from the kitchen broom. But he held back, perhaps afraid of the new form his obsession was taking – to be blunt, the same necrophilia which Heathcliff displays in Loyal's favourite scene in *Wuthering Heights* when he opens his beloved's grave. He was a shade too young to entertain such a giant passion quite though yet, Gabrielle. Gabrielle. Gabrielle Volets – as his hands wandered over the marble, and shutting his eyes, he felt the angel's scissor cutting off Gabrielle's hair – oh he wept at the necessity for that, how he longed to wrestle with the angel and cut off *his* long luxuriant hair. This became a recurring daydream – not exactly the healthiest one a young fellow in his mid-teens might nourish although, of course, one of his friends at school candidly confessed to imagining scenarios for lawless connections with contemporary women and girls that were so bestial, the effect of his friend's fantasies was to drive him back to the girl made out of letters incised on marble.

One day, Mr Kearns, his history teacher, one of the very few to have been shown the gravestone, pointed out to Loyal that the cutter of the stone had signed his masterpiece.

As Loyal lay down on the secret place in the orchard behind the smoke house where he had buried the stone, he would speak French to Gabrielle – she must have spoken it, and he could imagine her accuracy and fluency and elegant accent compared to his uncertainties about 'oeuf' and such squirmy things as cedillas and accents grave and circonflexes.

She had died when she was nineteen – had she ever thought of taking the veil – well, better not – considering the fate of the nun in *Maria Monk* although perhaps that was just the convents in Montreal. Did she read Catholic authors such as Dante Gabriel Rossetti – *The Blessed Damozel*, or, of course she could have been brought up on Miss Rossetti's *Goblin Market*. Fortunately, perhaps, Loyal knew not of Evelyn Waugh or Claudel as yet. Then, he thought – no, what would she read in French? *Pierrille*? Their grade nine novel *en français*? Would she have helped the housekeeper starch her brother's clerical collars? Or fallen in love with a local farm boy his age and....

Taking a spade, always kept handy, Loyal uncovered his beloved and hoisted it on top of himself, then when this proved rather too painful, just leaned against the smokehouse with the gravestone in his arms.

The first step was half taken – to see the exquisite forever hidden personality. Before this turned into burning passion for physical contact, there came a moment when he grew tired of his mania and threw the boring, irritating, heavy stone out of his bedroom window for yes, it had come to that – but – the remorseless stone did not break. If only it had. Swearing his friend of the candid confessions to secrecy, they both with flashlight and a muffled lantern met at two o'clock in the morning with sharpened spades and dug where the sexton's records and probings showed Gabrielle must lie. The priest's dog kept playfully tugging at their trousers to come and play with him or help him hunt rabbits, but so intent were they on their quest that they hardly noticed his increasingly sharper nippings and even quite dangerous barkings.

Thud!

Carefully remembering to pile the earth on one side away from the sods they would tamp down when they had finished with her, they suddenly caught a glimpse of Gabrielle's coffin plate.

Gabrielle Volets
Died August 7th 1900
Aged 19 years 5 months three days

His pal held the lantern now unmuffled and with one sweep, Loyal's prying bar opened the coffin lid like the cover of an old liturgical book.

There she lay looking up at them – dressed in white with blue sash, a locket around her throat, radiant face, golden hair, hands crossed on her breast, white prayer book, her eyes closed, her lips carmined. A silver locket at her throat. A mysterious bundle of muslin lay beside her – rather swaddled looking.

Then, in a trice, the fair maiden turned into dust – until the coffin seemed filled with brownish substance neither sawdust nor earth, even the dress dissolving and the hair. Only the locket – which now becoming a grave robber, his pal grabbed and handed over to Loyal.

A light came on in the rectory.

Closing the dread book, tears streaming down his face, Loyal and his friend calmly scraped the dirt back, keeping an eye on the window, then the sods were carefully fitted back.

Cleverly laid out in the order in which they were raised so that when Father Dewan came out in the moring to investigate that part of the cemetery where he thought he had distinguished some figures up to something, his short-sighted little eyes saw only a level seamless green turf with no hint of the anguish and beauty and blue sash once below.

The two young 'men' stayed up talking till dawn – for they, after that night, could no longer be said to be innocent boys; they opened and re-opened the locket but each time it revealed only the portrait of an older man, coarse-mouthed, handsome, slippery-eyed, his hair parted in the middle, his moustache and nose somehow suggestive of convenient nonchalances. Taking the clipped carte de visite out of its frame, they found scrawled on the back: 'Mon très best ami.'

The next few weeks were early summer with warm weather; a new development was, when swimming in the creek, to take the dread marble beloved with him and, lying on the sand in the shallow water, push it ahead of him till in the deeper water it plummeted him to the very bottom of the swimming hole, often, since he found it hard to let go, within an ace of drowning him. Perhaps this was part of his intention. After many dives and the assistance of a rope he had brought along for the purpose, he would retrieve from the deep water the marble message stone so long hidden in the brown sawdust and other dusts of the former summer kitchen.... Still in the water, he would press against the marble with his body a giant, blind hand that could sense the shapes of the letters that spoke her name with his breast, trace the angel cropping her hair with his belly, and braille the capital G in her Christian name with that part of himself most apt to obey the commands of the God of Touch.

Meanwhile Mr Kearns, journeying especially to Ailsa Craig to investigate the stonecutter's records there, was successful in finding the price paid for the carving from the design book especially prepared for members of a certain occult society, in this case the widow of a Grand Master. But the lady for whom the carving was ordered went to a distant place and died there to be buried under a convenient locally made memorial. Therefore, a pencilled note informed Mr Kearns that for a cut-rate price and hurriedly, the headstone was adapted to its new customer, a nineteen-year-old girl.

Mr Kearns next took the train over to London, and having written ahead to ensure permission, asked at the Diocesan Chancery to see what records remained of Fr. Volets and the household at his rectory.... He was not allowed direct access but he was told by a priestly clerk that Fr. Volets had not been removed to Paincourt by Bishop Walsh, but had been excommunicated for heresy. He and his housekeeper, a sister, ended their days with a family in Sandwich and were buried there. Fr. Volets's niece died after giving birth to a stillborn baby born out of wedlock. Unnoted by her recent resurrectionist, her child lay beneath the blue sash swaddled in muslin – little wanderer through Eternity and Time who had ended his journey in the latter, first at St. Anthony's Chapel graveyard, and then that of St. Joseph's to be there pulverized again by two mad young men intent on the pursuit of love and beauty even unto the Gates of Hell and the remotest part of the Kingdom of Shadows.

Mr Kearns, closing his notebook, staggered out of the Chancery archives, lay down under a huge sycamore tree.

No! He should tell him to break the evil spell before it was too late, and so, he hurried to a streetcar route to get to the station as soon as possible. Alas, he missed the last train that might have carried him to Bornish before nightfall, and in panic, he determined simply to walk, a determination that brought him to his house shortly before dawn.

That night Loyal had slept with his beloved petrified as he had every night for the last two years and he had not yet awakened when Mr Kearns knocked on the farmhouse door, the front one, never used, except for funerals, so that Mrs O'Hanley who was up but had lost her glasses momentarily, took her time answering his knock. By that time, he had come to his senses and was rapping on the kitchen door.

'Oh Mr Kearns. I think I recognize you – aren't you Loyal's history master? I've mislaid my spectacles. He always speaks so highly of you, come in and have some breakfast with us. Some tea?'

'Perhaps later, Mrs O'Hanley, after – there's something I've got to tell Loyal immediately.'

Mrs O'Hanley thought about this for a while. Then she beckoned Mr Kearns to follow her upstairs.

'Bring your notebook along with you – I know how you scholars get sudden flashes of inspiration that must be shared right away while they're still fresh – I'll knock on his door first, because you see, once I opened it without warning and I surprised him trying to draw of portrait of himself bare naked ... Mad lad, he is.'

A permissive murmur seemed to answer the mother's knocking.

Like the cover of a familiar book, a novel, the door opened.

A young woman dressed in blue sash and white muslin dress stood up from the bed where she had been lounging.

'Hein, hein?' she twanged. *'Qu'est que c'est le truc?'*

On the bed where she had been lounging, lay a gravestone, plain, elegantly lettered in Baskerville, a skull with enormous wings projecting on either side of it carved at the top of the stone.

Darting to the window, which she raised with an abrupt screech of resisting wood, the young woman turned her back on her visitors because she had caught sight of the pig stable.

'Impossible – la chapelle plein de cochons, son of a bitch. *Pauvre oncle – cochons, cochons.'* After a wild bumping-into-things and a race through the house, downstairs and upstairs, they saw her re-emerge in the barnyard, when they could tear their eyes away from the bed, and there she entered the pig stable which had once been a place where mass was said and

soon pigs were pouring out, some of them returning to give battle since she was disturbing their meal time wait rituals.

Loyal's father entered the room, having just awakened, and focused on his wife, her hands gliding over the letters on his son's tombstone, and the letters read, suddenly deafening all in the room to the terrible racket erupting in waves from the Pig Chapel:

Loyal O'Hanley
Died August 7th 1936
Aged 19 years 5 months three days
Born Lot 39
Concession XII
West Williams
Ontario
Canada
North America
The New World
The British Empire
The Earth
The Milky Way
The Stars

The Car

THE FARM WHERE BERT LIVED was about three miles from the town and every day, except in the very hardest part of the winter, he went in and out to the high school on his bicycle. There were two miles of lane and side road; then another mile of open highway. People knew what time it was by his bicycle going across a window. Old Mrs Nau would wave to him from her sun porch in the morning. In December, when it gets dark so early, he would say hello to Mrs Nau as he met her carrying a lantern walking home from her sister's place farther down the road and he was coming home from school. Next, there was the gravel side road and Dennis Schmidt waved to him as he crossed the yard carrying a pail of oyster shells to his hen house. In late February. Past Schmidt's house, and just before the railway tracks there was a small, weather-beaten cottage where a kid of four or five was always playing in the mud or snow of his mother's laneway. David looked harsh – there was hardly enough face to go around for all the harshness in that invisible heart. Bert had tried to be friends with him, and had only succeeded in learning his first name, but, lately, David always threw stones so Bert had to ride by very quietly and very fast. Still, Bert could see what David was always playing with – a broken toy car. But before he could identify its make, David would reach for a stone.

Up over the railway tracks and whiz down beside the dark fir grove and then a small seven-acre pond that bordered on his father's farm. In the rushes where the lake almost touched the road there was the rusty skeleton of an ancient car. In spring, a wild swan came to nest there. Then up another hill past a culvert where there was great fun damming the freshet in April and then down a long lane.

There was another country boy, Keith McNamara who rode in on his bike too, but Bert never rode in with him. So far as other bikes were concerned, he always managed to have the highway alone to himself. When he was alone he could say over his lessons to himself, or watch things or just be a bicycle. Mostly, he watched things: the colour of tree branches, pigeons on a barn roof in the sun, grass along the fence bottom; the sun on a frozen puddle over in a field. The rain beating down on a toy car in the mud. The gravel on the road.

In the summer, Bert's bicycle wouldn't be seen so much since he'd be at home working. Nor would the kid be visible so much either. There was an abandoned auto graveyard across the road from the woman's house where he played in the summer a lot. Bert, as he wheeled in to his music lesson or to the library, positively missed the welcoming pebble. But then the kid not being there meant he could look at an old log that stuck up through the gravel; this old log (bump!) was a relic of the days when the first pathmaster of the township had made a corduroy road there out of tree trunks.

On a hot bright early July, he had slowed down over the log when he saw the kid's mother coming over to him from her clothes line. Her face was brown and rather smart looking; her hair was hidden in a piece of bright cloth almost like a turban. He could hear the kid making automobile sounds in one of the wrecked cars across the ditch. You could probably only bear to sit on the old seats when the sun had really dried them out. With grass in the windshield the woman's son sat humming about the invisible journey his 1922 Essex without wheels took him on, or his 1928 Durant with blinds on the windows in the back you could pull down. Did the invisible car lights shine on wet night pavement going up a hill, the boy humming and sputtering to himself?

THE CAR

His mother said, 'Do you want a piece?'

Bert looked up with a start. She had come out right to him and she meant him. Then he knew what she meant. He knew what she meant and also what meant the dozens of car tracks in her laneway, or sometimes a car still there in the morning, or two cars once in the afternoon, the two cars not the same and the whole bunch of cars not the same, even a Michigan licence once. He knew what she meant before she pointed to what she meant on herself. Suddenly, she was up close, her fingers on his fly. Breaking away, he could hear her laughing behind him. The sput sput sounds from the auto graveyard had stopped.

For a month after this, the grass and cloud and branch shapes stopped. He even thought of going to the library some other way. It was because he hadn't thought much about that like that before. It seemed part of the car world, not the bicycle world. The cars that blurred by on the highway were driven by young men with their girl friends moved over close beside them. And then his bicycle dream came back to him, and once more he could see the countless shapes of pebble, leaf and grass. The two wheels of his bicycle always reminded him of the map of the two hemispheres at school. He rode through the stars with the New World and the Old World for wheels.

❦ ❦ ❦

'What happened to your forehead, Bert?' asked his friend Tom. Tom lived in a dingy old double house on Shakespeare Street near the railway station. They were up in his bedroom in the middle of a heap of things to do with marionettes. Things they had been sewing, scenes they had been painting and the theatre itself lit with the aid of an evil-smelling old car battery which Tom, who was interested in electricity, had rigged up.

'That kid that lives in the funny house, he got me with a stone this morning. Didn't you notice it before?'

'Nah. We've been so busy. Sewing. Ouch! I've pricked myself again. Bert, what we need is a thimble! Yeah. Sewing. And one thing and another.' Tom started to laugh. Really giggle. Sometimes they got laughing so that Tom's grandmother said they'd both die of heart attacks. And once after a really prolonged fit of giggles, Bert had heard an indignant voice say sharply through the wall from somewhere in the house on the other side ... 'Oh, the fool!'

The Young People's at the Anglican Church had asked them to put on their marionettes and they had been working at them spare evenings since Christmas.

'What's this funny house?'

'It's a brothel, I guess.'

'Sh! Hush, Bert!' Tom's grandmother who usually sat up crocheting afghans in her bedroom had extremely sharp ears for this sort of thing. Work at the marionettes languished now for about a quarter of an hour as this naturally interesting topic was quietly explored. The fingers, the woman's fingers on Bert's privates, was received with blushes and awe. Then Bert, putting his needle into a marionette, said it was late and a long way to ride home.

'Why don't you stay here?'

'It's too late to phone them and ask, you know.'

'But don't they wait up for you anyhow?'

'Yeah. They sleep light. When I get home they sleep heavy.'

'Aren't you afraid to ride home all alone at night?'

'N – oh. I'm not.'

'Gee, I would.'

'If there's a moon and clouds, why, it's just beautiful, Tom. And the highway's all to yourself.'

'Well, there's no moon tonight,' said Tom, looking down at

THE CAR

the street light through the branches outside his window.

Tom went down with Bert and let him out the front door. He watched Bert swing up on the bike or rather watched him put the whole machine in between his legs as if it were an attachment to his body like a hat or a boot. And then watched him dwindle away down the street by the railway sheds. The street lamps batted his shadow back and forth. They lengthened it, doubled it and shortened it on the wet March pavement. A cat crossed the street. There was a new car parked across the road. Tom supposed it was someone visiting at the house two doors down where there was an old lady had her brother visiting her from Detroit.

Out on the highway there were no more street lights and Bert's eyes met the darkness directly. There was a small light in a distant farmhouse. He used that light for all it was worth to judge the distance by. Somebody waiting for their people to come home. At a certain break in the woodlots that ranged themselves around the horizon he should be able to see the yard light at home which they'd have left on for him. But the break never came. A dog barked at him. Far away another dog barked at that dog.

He kept sharpening at his ears in case he should hear the wheels going off the asphalt and onto the shoulder. There were one or two unrailed culverts you could fall over. And then his eyes began to work with the darkness better or was it that some light broke through the thick low cloud? There was supposed to be a full moon up above the clouds.

Every forward tread of his feet up the pedals and down pulled the shapes of things towards him: posts, snow fence, trees, roof peaks. He could hear thaw water dripping from the roof of the Nau sun porch. He judged where their mailbox must be and swung out. He began to sing to himself. It was just a rod or two to the side road now and he would be safe. There hadn't been a car yet going either way on the highway so why was he thinking that? Because there was a car coming. It didn't have any headlights on.

Since he himself didn't have a light he couldn't be sure right away where he was on the highway. After swinging out for the mailbox he had lost all sense of the highway's edge. He turned at right angles and deliberately pumped into the gravel shoulder, but he couldn't seem to do it. He couldn't get it to sound under his tires. Was he going at a long slant ... he must have been, for just as the roaring sound of the car was right at his ears, the gravel and sand crunched and he fell. But just before he fell into the ditch, the car brushed him with its air flow, its oily smell. Even in the no-light he could see where the driver should be and the driver's wheel sticking up. Was it that there was no driver or that the driver was crouching down so as not to be seen? Or that the driver was dead, or that the car was driverless? The roaring whirring sound of the car petered out and he walked his bike to the side road where he swung on and raced for home.

At first he was terribly afraid. He had never been so close to death before. There wasn't any car at the woman's house. At the end of his father's lane where the trees arched their boughs over and made a tunnel of darkness, and where most people would have been afraid, his fear left him. It was as if it had not really happened. Upstairs in his bedroom, he took off his pant clips and felt tired through. Tired in a new way as if he had ridden many more miles than he really had. The brush with the grey blind car had known where to suck at his energy, to get at the very source of his being. It was like the turbaned woman. For a few moments. He rolled into bed in just his shirt. He listened to the Japanese cuckoo clock ticking above his bed that his mother had given him for Christmas. The ticking retreated, then stopped. When it stopped then he knew that he was just about to fall asleep. He could just tell by the window that the moon had finally come out through the clouds.

THE CAR

In the morning he knew that he was almost awake when he could not hear the clock, and when he was really awake he could hear the clock and it was almost time to go to school.

During the spare that day at school, the willowy boy from St Luke's Young People's who had originally asked them if they would put on their marionettes got up from his desk. He was only fifteen but already tall with a heavy shave shadow although not filled out yet in either face or body. He watched Ronald coming up the row towards him. He said he had completely forgotten, but of course it was Lent still and they couldn't have the marionette show until Lent was over. It was a fall night in early October before Tom and Bert did show their marionettes at St Luke's. Before that, three things happened.

❦ ❦ ❦

In May, on a day after a big storm old Mr Nau beckoned to Bert as he rode home from school. He propped his bicycle against the mailbox and followed the humped old man into the two-room cottage crowded with things that shook and rattled every time a truck or a Greyhound bus went by.

Mrs Nau lay in the centre of a big double bed.

Bert leaned down close to her so as to catch what she was trying to tell him.

No one was quite sure what had happened, but in walking down the traffic, against the traffic, with her lantern, from her sister's place, Mrs Nau had been knocked down apparently by a hit-and-run driver. That morning Bert had seen a piece of her lantern caught in the fence. The rest of the lantern had been pressed into her hand which was heavily bandaged. But they had given up bandaging her.

'What is she trying to tell me?' Bert asked Mr Nau. He bent down again. Her face was old but very smooth. Her glasses had perfectly round shiny steel rims. Like the wheels of a glass bicycle. Then he did catch what she was saying.

'No, Mrs Nau. I don't ride about very much at night. Besides I've got a light on my bicycle now.' He leaned closer. 'I've got a light on my bicycle now.'

Behind the glasses she closed her eyes and smiled slightly. With its hundred shades and colours the quilt on the bed leapt up at him. Dresses as far back as sixty years had gone into it. He knew he should be afraid. She knew something and was trying to save him. After all her lantern and her walking against the traffic had not saved her from a car that must have crossed the road to get her from behind.

While he was eating his supper and looking out the west windows at the sun yellowing behind great masses of blue-grey clouds breaking up as the cold weather was and flying into the east, his mother came from the telephone to tell him that Mrs Nau was dead.

Yet, after a few weeks he was not even sure that it had been an accident with a car that had killed Mrs Nau. Had it not been really that she was terribly old and had fallen down by the roadside. Bert lived in a dream bubble whose tough gelatinous sides not even the woman at the cottage with her turban or the old woman dying could break into. Nor even his own experience with the mysterious car although it had really been most since that experience that he had felt the dream bubble thicken around him as tortoises grow a thicker shell the summer of the great fierce sun.

June came and he was writing his Middle School examinations. The wild roses were out at the end of the lane. He took some to the sick room of the hatchery man whose wife had come out to ask if he would visit her husband, not just leave the flowers.

'Sure, I've got time,' said Bert leaning his bike up against one of the big willows by the Schmidts' gate.

'He's watched you go by every day and there's something

he wants to speak to you about.' Bert had noticed that the pattern of her house dress had been represented by a patch on Mrs Nau's quilt. They must have worked on the quilt together and there had been scraps left over when this dress was sewed.

After Mrs Schmidt showed him up to her husband's room, she had to go out again to the large shed at the back where the chickens were kept. Some baby chicks must be in the kitchen, perhaps even in the cellar. He could hear them chirping in mounting furry squeaking waves like masses of chokecherry blossoms waving in the wind down the lane.

Mr Schmidt was propped up on some pillows and was looking out at the fresh morning sunlight. From his window you could see the dark fir grove that hid the lake and low down in front of it the cottage where the woman lived. The Schmidts, Bert noticed, slept in separate rooms and did not have any children.

'You've come, Bert.'

Bert went over close to him and took his bandaged hand for a moment.

'How are you feeling, Mr Schmidt?'

Mr Schmidt said that he was through.

'Do you want to see how I'm through? Just take down the covers and look at my side.'

Bert, his hands trembling, did as he was told, and after the man's nightshirt had been scrunched up, he saw the bandages on the side. They smelled slightly. Above and below the bandage great welts and deep scratches backed up, turned and looped. These were healing but they drove and tracked to gorings underneath the bandaging that would never heal.

'What happened, Mr Schmidt?'

He seemed to hear him say that there had been a car parked across the Schmidts' lane one night. He had gone out to tell them to move away when the car caught him with its car handle and moved slowly off dragging him for about forty feet before he fell off.

Outside a train whistled. It was the morning freight from the town slowly picking up speed as it came out of the yards. Five minutes ago it would have been moving its orange, pink, yellow and dark red oblongs in front of Tom's house where his grandmother would be watching it through the foam of her lace curtains. Like postage stamps on old letters.

'Do you know where the car comes from?' asked Mr Schmidt, suddenly taking hold of Bert's arm.

'No, I don't, Mr Schmidt.'

'It hit old Mother Nau and run. And it hit me and run. It is somebody who visits her place.'

'Whose place?'

'There. Out the window there. Do you ever visit her?'

'No, Mr Schmidt.'

'She ever ask you?'

'Once, Mr Schmidt.'

'Did you go in unto her?' Bert shook his head. 'She'll get you like she's got me.'

'But how did she get you?'

Mr Schmidt lay back on his pillow. The words he had been saying had tired him out. He whispered.

'She's going to kill that kid of hers some day too. Once he came over here – early in the morning, three o'clock, told us his mother had locked him out. When we took him back she cursed at him. I didn't want to leave him there.' Mrs Schmidt was coming up the stairs. 'Be careful of her ... of going by there at night. First you'll dream of her as I did and then she'll put her claw ... in your side.'

Mrs Schmidt came in with the wild roses. She had put them in a milk jug whose handle was broken off. It was time for Bert to go in to his examination.

On the way back he saw the doctor's car at Schmidt's

house. At the woman's house there was a locked-up, deserted feeling. Perhaps they'd gone away. The kid's toy car lay on its back in the mud. The bicycle bumped over the corduroy log. A rat crossed the road on its way into the auto graveyard. The sky was blue and the sun a noontide white yellow.

But once he was over the railway tracks and the air rushed up against him as he sped down the hill, the lake glittering, the new green of the leaves, he was safe in a different country and he really couldn't believe that it had been a car that had killed both Mrs Nau and Mr Schmidt. Hadn't it been that they were old or ill anyhow? He knew that some day he would have to know for sure either way. But not now. He couldn't be serious about it now school was just about over and summer was coming on.

The sun set farther north each day. The wild roses disappeared. Other flowers took their place in the lane. The lane itself grew dusty and white, grasses blossomed, hardened and tasselled with their seeds. His face and arms were sun-burnt from working in the fields at haying, hoeing turnips and harvesting wheat. The sun began to set further south again.

All he used his bicycle for now was to go in for library books. At the end of the lane unable to wait any longer he would lie down in the grass and start reading the books. Reading in that happiest of all lights – half-past-five summer sunlight.

❦ ❦ ❦

'You saw him before he died then?'

'When he was dying his mother phoned me he wanted to see me. He used to ride in to school from his farm the same time I would, but I would never ride with him. I don't know why.'

'But wasn't he instantly killed, and found dead in the road?'

Bert didn't know what to say to that. The lights and the waxed floor of his music teacher's studio seemed suddenly too bright for him. Things swung about a bit. Did she see something in his face that he didn't? Was he marked out for some special terror and had he already talked to three people when they were freshly dead? Had his bicycle been for some time leading him into that country one always suspected of just possibly existing: the Kingdom of Shadows where things disappeared the moment you turned your back upon them and the Republic of Darkness where at the edge of the swamp people came to dump things or make the two-backed beast and at the end of a stubby dead-end lane there waited an empty car, an empty rusted skeleton.

'No,' he said, smiling. 'You must have just heard that. He lived for a week after his accident. I talked to him.'

'But aren't you afraid?'

'No.'

'Well, why aren't you?'

'Because nothing's going to happen to me.'

❦ ❦ ❦

'Why won't you stay at my place?' asked Tom as they walked out in the leafless fall night. They were taking the marionettes home to Tom's. Tom carried a box filled with them. Bert had some more in a box on his carrier. 'Well, why won't you?'

'I don't know. I've never been a night away from home except once at the Toronto Exhibition. And that was with them. I've just got to get home, that's all.'

He was walking with his bicycle. He changed over his bike so it wouldn't be between them.

'You're an idiot, Bert.'

'I know it. I can't help it. I am.'

A car with one headlight rolled down the brick paved hill

THE CAR

and across the iron bridge. In the doorway of one of the old houses on Waterloo Street a pair of lovers were saying goodnight. He looked over at his friend, who had not seen them. He listened to Tom's voice which had not completely changed yet. From some corner of his mind – perhaps where a child played in a muddy lane rutted with the tires of a hundred different cars – there floated up the notion that they were both boxes of marionettes for in their secret parts lurked Calcutta millions of potential heirs. And the couple in the doorway were the theatre. He resented the fact that the couple in the doorway could pull someone like himself or Tom into the world without permission asked.

'I'll never get married,' he suddenly blurted out to Tom.

'Why not?'

'Oh, I just won't. I hate it.'

Eventually the doctors' houses, schools public and schools separate, convents, churches and factory fronts and always smaller houses unravelled themselves into Tom's house where Bert put his box of marionettes on the porch.

'You won't stay?' said Tom.

'No, I won't stay,' said Bert, beginning to wobble away on his bicycle. Tom stood out watching him until he turned off behind the ice house.

The light on his bicycle proceeded into the darkness. It joggled down and up with the invisible wheels behind it. The bicycle light had a blue-white colour and sharp fine rays stuck out from it like a thistledown of ice. The sky was completely overcast although far away to the northeast there was a red glow where a barn or a house in another township was burning down. The reflection of the town's lights from the single cloud above was bright enough to guide him down the first part of the highway. The cold air was thick as water and it had to be cut through with an effort.

So he came to the turn-off and the gravel road. A dog barked in the hollow distance. He got as far as Schmidt's gateway before he sensed the lightless car turn out from the woman's place and soundlessly gather speed toward him. He pointed the bicycle into the ditch and felt the air stream ripple over him. It had missed him as it had before. Stubbornly he lifted his bike up onto the road and wheeled as far as the cottage. He could hear the car backing up and turning around beneath the willow trees at Schmidt's place.

He turned into her yard and threw himself at her porch. No answer come to his knock except the resentful silence of deserted spaces. The door opened just with his knocking. He reached down for his bicycle and pulled it up into the doorway. Of course the car came into the yard but the turn sapped at its speed so it had to go straight out into the field behind the yard before it could get up enough force to smash the house. A chunk of dirt spun out from its back wheel and hit him on the forehead. Always until now he had hoped that the other cases were genuine accidents. There was no doubt now that they weren't. The house wood shrieked and splintered as the car hit it on the other side. He could hear the car backing up for another charge.

As the car pushed the house right over he got out of reach with his bicycle and he was climbing the road up to the railroad as the car finished knocking the house down. Then it paused, its motor purring. It was wondering where he was. He ducked down as his wheels rattled over the wooden crossing and the railway crossing sign showed up against the sky. But he hadn't thought of turning off the light in time.

As he began to roll down the hill beside the fir grove he could hear the car snapping the fence wire, crunching the gravel on the railway embankment and then tearing through

THE CAR

the grove with the force of a great wind. He could hear trees snapping off and a frightened animal bolted up over the road.

There was a lane came out of the grove and as he passed it the car, which had finally turned its lights on, would deliberately and easily blot him out. Bert was conscious of hearing himself screaming and of something rising up like black water to his mouth, now to his nostrils and inevitably to his eyes. As he turned back and pumped himself up over the railway track it rose over his mouth. He'd got as far as the woman's laneway before he could make it stop.

For it was no use trying to escape the car. It would get him just before Schmidt's laneway. And it was no use getting off and running across the fields. It would particularly enjoy that. There was but one thing to try and that was to meet it full on. If it were just a car it would kill him. If it were more than a car, why more than just what he was now might be its match. He remembered the sunlight on the dust at the end of the lane and reading in some library book that ghosts were as frightened of us as we were of them.

So he turned round. He turned on the bicycle light. Like slowly opening eyelids the headlights came up over the railway crossing and the x of the crossing sign seemed an evil standard held in one hand by a masked commander. He pumped as fast as he could toward it. It rolled across and down toward him, but as he got closer it stopped and then began to back up. It changed as he changed. The early morning freight was now coming by the next crossing and gave a long warning whistle. What the car was trying to do was pin Bert to the centre of the crossing so the train would get him. The one yellow staring eye of the train attracted him just before his front wheel touched the first plank of the crossing.

The trained rushed between them filling the horror between them. Between the freight cars he could see the lights. Then it played its last trick ... Just before the caboose, the car had vanished. He could see through the moving crack the emptiness and he fell forward in a faint, his head and hands within inches of the wheels.

Bert's father had, upon rising, looked in Bert's room and then driven out immediately to look for him. At the crossing he saw his son sprawled on top of his bicycle, his hands reaching toward the tracks. As he lifted him up, Bert woke up. In streaks of pink and light brown the dawn was leaning out of the eastern sky.

'Dad,' Bert said, his teeth chattering. 'We've got to go into the junk yard there and look at one of the cars. I dreamt and I know he's in it. Do me this one favour. Don't be mad at me for not getting home. I tried to get home. I tried to get home.'

His father took his hand, after they had put Bert's bicycle on the shoulder of the road, and together they jumped over the dry ditch filled with pitchfork burs and crouched through a loose board into the auto graveyard.

Two acres of rustling wheelless dreariness. A short path that had worn grass and weeds down led to a car in which someone sat at the steering wheel. Bert ran over and leaned down to look in.

The woman's boy sat steering the wheelless car. His eyes could not see the road that he was driving because the rats had stolen them. But still the steering wheel clutched his hands because the bindweed growing up from underneath the car fastened them there with many a withered convolvular twining. And had fastened them there since early that summer.

Bert, on the doctor's advice, was kept in bed several days. He cried a great deal and then a mood of sadness would freeze not only his tears but all of the life springs within him. On the second day he got up, went over to his homework table by the stovepipe and searched in his pencil box until he found a certain pen he had been given as a child. It was a short wooden

THE CAR

pen with a round fluted glass nib tapering to a point. He dipped it in his ink bottle and wrote the following:

Once there was a boy named David. His mother was a whore. He had a different father every night and from his crib which he still slept in he heard and saw unspeakable things. So he spent most of his time outside playing with a toy car in the dirt. He kept imagining he was in the car and it was a big powerful car like the ones the men had who came to use his mother. Then in the car wrecker's yard he used to sit whole days in a car that couldn't run, but he'd pretend it could. He was a flower filled with pus.

In the hot-smelling rank weed jungle, he hated. He dreamed of killing with his car. He hated the boy who went by because he heard the mother ask him for free and he knew the boy half would have. So he hummed and dreamed to himself and at night when he was asleep he was given a big powerful car and he sped up and down the whole world with it – killing whoever he pleased. But the boy he hated got away.

And he couldn't seem to get his mother's customers in their soiled linen and their fast cars. But he could get those who walked or bicycled. If they had been kind to you that made the killing better and felt relief for a while. He loved his mother and she killed him. She killed the man within him. That is what would die if you saw your mother arched over by the pushing, grunting men.

So he – the boy, David – killed the old woman, and the man. Both of these had been kind to him when he used to run away, and then the other boy on a bicycle. And then he tried at the marionette boy on the bicycle again.

Oh poor ghost of a poor child, all last summer a yellow burdock grew up between your legs and bindweed was a crown for you and a chain until I pushed you back into hell or on into paradise.

Or on the road you drive is there suddenly a bed pushed across it like a tail gate on which lie a man a woman and you smash out of their bodies to reappear once more among us, a giant child in a spiritual car whose teeth we have sharpened and unto whose wheels we have added scythes and sickles.

    Bert wiped the pen and laid it down on the paper. Then from the pocket of his shirt he took the toy car. It had been discarded forever in the mud of the laneway. He put it on top of what he had written.

    Then he lay down on the bed and hid his face.

    The cuckoo clock began to tick again and his hand fingered his bicycle clip hanging on the railing at the top of his bed.

The Bully

AS A CHILD I lived on a farm not far from a small town called Partridge. In the countryside about Partridge, thin roads of gravel and dust slide in and out among the hollows and hills. As roads go, they certainly aren't very brave, for quite often they go round a hill instead of up it and even in the flattest places they will jog and hesitate absurdly. But then this latter tendency often comes from some blunder a surveying engineer made a hundred years ago. And although his mind has long ago dissolved, its forgetfulness still pushes the country people crooked where they might have gone straight.

Some of the farmhouses on these ill-planned roads are made of red brick and have large barns and great cement silos and soft large strawstacks behind them. And other farmhouses are not made of brick, but of frame and clapboard that gleam with the silver film unpainted wood attains after years of wild rain and shrill wind beating upon it. The house where I was born was such a place, and I remember that whenever it rained, from top to bottom the whole outside of the house would turn jet-black as if it were blushing in shame or anger.

Perhaps it blushed because of my father who was not a very good farmer. He was what is known as an afternoon farmer. He could never get out into the fields till about half-past eleven in the morning and he never seemed to be able to grow much of anything except buckwheat which as everyone knows is the lazy farmer's crop. If you could make a living out of playing checkers and talking, then my father would have made enough to send us all to college, but as it was he did make enough to keep us alive, to buy tea and coffee, cake and pie, boots and stockings, and a basket of peaches once every summer. So it's really hard to begrudge him a few games of checkers or a preference for talking instead of a preference for ploughing.

When I was six, my mother died of T.B. and I was brought up by my Aunt Coraline and by my two older sisters, Noreen and Kate. Noreen, the oldest of us, was a very husky, lively girl. She was really one of the liveliest girls I have ever seen. She rode every horse we had bare-back, sometimes not with a bridle at all but just by holding on to their manes. When she was fifteen, in a single day she wall-papered both our kitchen and our living-room. And when she was sixteen she helped my father draw in hay just like a hired man. When she was twelve she used to tease me an awful lot. Sometimes when she had teased me too much, I would store away scraps of food for days, and then go off down the side road with the strong idea in my head that I was not going to come back. But then Noreen and Kate would run after me with tears in their eyes and, having persuaded me to throw away my large collection of breakfast toast crusts and agree to come back, they would both promise never to tease me again. Although Kate, goodness knows, had no need to promise that for she was always kind, would never have thought of teasing me. Kate was rather like me in being shy and in being rather weak. Noreen's strength and boldness made her despise Kate and me, but she was like us in some ways. For instance Noreen had a strange way of feeding the hens. Each night she would sprinkle the grain out on the ground in the shape of a letter or some other pattern, so that when the hens ate the grain, they were forced to spell out Noreen's initials or to form a cross and a circle. There were just enough hens to make this rather an interesting game. Sometimes, I know, Noreen spelt out whole sentences in this way, a letter or two each night, and often wondered to whom she was writing up in the sky.

Aunt Coraline, who brought me up, was most of the time

sick in bed and as a result was rather pettish and ill-tempered. In the summer time, she would spend most of the day in her room making bouquets out of any flowers we could bring her; even dandelions, shepherd's purse, or Queen Anne's lace. She was very skillful at putting letters of the alphabet into a bouquet, with two kinds of flowers, you know, one for the letters and one for the background. Aunt Coraline's room was filled with all sorts of jars and bottles containing bouquets, some of them very ancient so that her room smelt up a bit, especially in the hot weather. She was the only one of us who had a room to herself. My father slept in the kitchen. Aunt Coraline's days were devoted to the medicine bottle and the pill box, making designs in bouquets, telling us stories, and bringing us up; her nights were spent in trying to get to sleep and crying softly to herself.

When we were children we never were worked to death, but still we didn't play or read books all of the time. In the summer we picked strawberries, currants, and raspberries. Sometimes we picked wild berries into milkpails for money, but after we had picked our pails full, before we could get the berries to the woman who had commissioned them, the berries would settle down in the pails and of course the woman would refuse then to pay what she had promised because we hadn't brought her full pails. Sometimes our father made us pick potato beetles off the potato plants. We would tap the plants on one side with a shingle and hold out a tin can on the other side to catch the potato bugs as they fell. And we went for cows and caught plough horses for our father.

Every Saturday night we children all took turns bathing in the dishpan and on Sundays, after Sunday school, we would all sit out on the lawn and drink the lemonade that my father would make in a big glass pitcher. The lemonade was always slightly green and sour like the moon when it's high up in a summer sky. While we were drinking the lemonade, we would listen to our Victrola gramophone which Noreen would carry out of the house along with a collection of records. These were all very old, very thick records and their names were: 'I Know Where the Flies Go', 'The Big Rock Candy Mountain', 'Hand Me Down My Walking Cane', and a dialogue about some people in a boarding-house that went like this:

'Why can't you eat this soup?'

Various praising replies about the soup and its fine, fine qualities by all the fifteen members of the boarding-house. Then:

'So WHY can't you eat this soup?'

And the non-appreciative boarder replies:

'Because I ain't got a spoon.'

Even if no one laughed, and of course we always did, the record company had thoughtfully put in some laughter just to fill up the centre. Those Sunday afternoons are all gone now and if I had known I was never to spend any more like them, I would have spent them more slowly.

We began to grow up. Noreen did so gladly but Kate and I secretly hated to. We were much too weak to face things as they were. We were weak enough to prefer what we had been as children rather than what we saw people often grew up to be, people who worked all day at dull, senseless things and slept all night and worked all day and slept all night and so on until they died. I think Aunt Coraline must have felt the same when she was young and decided to solve the problem by being ill. Unfortunately for us, neither Kate nor I could quite bring ourselves to take this line. I don't know what Kate decided, but at the age of eleven I decided that school-teaching looked neither too boring nor too hard so a school-teacher I would be. It was my one chance to escape what my father had fallen into. To become a teacher one had to go to high school five years and go one year to normal school. Two miles away in the town of Partridge there actually stood a high school.

It was not until the summer after I had passed my entrance examination that I began to feel rather frightened of the new life ahead of me. That spring, Noreen had gone into town to work for a lady as a housemaid. At my request, she went to look at the high school. It was situated right next the jail, and Noreen wrote home that of the two places she'd much rather go to the jail, even although they had just made the gates of the jail three feet higher. Of that summer I particularly remember one sultry Sunday afternoon in August when I walked listlessly out to the mailbox and, leaning against it, looked down the road in the general direction of town. The road went on past our house and then up a hill and then not over the top of the hill for it went crooked a bit, wavered and disappeared, somehow, on the other side. Somewhere on that road stood a huge building which would swallow me up for five years. Why I had ever wanted to leave all the familiar things around me, I could hardly understand. Why people had to grow up and leave home I could not understand either. I looked first at the road and then into the dull sky as I wondered at this. I tried to imagine what the high school would really be like, but all I could see or feel was a strong tide emerging from it to sweep me into something that would give me a good shaking up.

Early every morning, I walked into high school with my lunch box and my schoolbooks under my arm. And I walked home again at night. I have none of the textbooks now that were used at that school, for I sold them when I left. And I can't remember very much about them except that the French book was fat and blue. One took fifteen subjects in all: business practice (in this you learnt how to write out cheques and pay electric light bills, a knowledge that so far has been of no use to me); there were English, geography, mathematics,

French, spelling, history, physical training, music, art, science (here one was taught how to light a Bunsen burner) and there must have been other subjects for I'm sure there were fifteen of them. I never got used to high school. There were so many rooms, so many people, so many teachers. The teachers were watchful as heathen deities and it was painful to displease them. Almost immediately I became the object of everyone's disgust and rage. The geography teacher growled at me, the English teacher stood me up in corners. The history teacher denounced me as an idiot. The French teacher cursed my accent. In physical training I fell off innumerable parallel-bars showing, as the instructor remarked, that I could not and never would co-ordinate my mind with my body. My platoon of the cadet corps discovered that the only way to make progress possible in drill was to place me deep in the centre of the ranks away from all key positions. In manual training I broke all sorts of precious saws and was soundly strapped for something I did to the iron-lathe. For no reason that I could see, the art teacher went purple in the face at me, took me out into the hall and struck my defenceless hands with a leather thong. The French teacher once put me out into the hall, a far worse fate than that of being put in a corner, for the halls were hourly stalked by the principal in search of game; anyone found in the halls he took off with him to his office where he administered a little something calculated to keep the receiver out of the halls thereafter.

Frankly, I must have been, and I was, a simpleton, but I did the silly things I did mainly because everyone expected me to do them. Very slowly I began to be able to control myself and give at least some sort of right answer when questioned. Each night when I came home at first, Kate would ask me how I liked high school. I would reply as stoutly as I could that I was getting on all right. But gradually I did begin to get along not too badly and might have been a little happy if something not connected with my studies had not thrown me back into a deeper misery.

This new unhappiness had something to do with the place where those students who came from the country ate their lunch. This place was called a cafeteria and was divided into a girls' cafeteria and a boys' one. After about a month of coming to the boys' cafeteria to eat my lunch, I noticed that a certain young man (he couldn't be called a boy) always sat near me with his back to me at the next long table. The cafeteria was a basement room filled with three long tables and rows of wire-mended chairs. Now my lunch always included a small bottle of milk. The bottle had originally been a vinegar bottle and was very difficult to drink from unless you put your head away back and gulped it fast. One day when I had finished my sandwiches and was drinking my milk, he turned around and said quietly: 'Does baby like his bottle?'

I blushed and immediately stopped drinking. Then I waited until he would finish his lunch and go away. While I waited with downcast eyes and a face red with shame, I felt a furious rush of anger against Kate and Aunt Coraline for sending milk for my lunch in a vinegar bottle. Finally, I began to see that he had finished his lunch and was not going to leave until I did. I put the vinegar bottle back in my lunch box and walked as quickly as I could out of the boys' cafeteria, upstairs into the classroom left open during the noon hour so that the country people could study there. He followed me there and sat in the seat opposite me with, what I managed to discover in the two times I looked at him, a derisive smile upon his face. He had a dark, swarthy, carved face and complexion, with heavy lips, and he wore a dark green shirt. With him sitting beside me, I had no chance of ever getting the products of New Zealand and Australia off by heart and so I failed the geography test we had that afternoon. Day after day he tormented me. He never hit me. He would always just stay close to me, commenting on how I ate my food or didn't drink my vinegar and once he pulled a chair from beneath me. Since our first meeting I never drank anything while he was near me. Between him and my friends the teachers, my life in first form at high school was a sort of Hell with too many tormenting fiends and not enough of me to go round so they could all get satisfaction. If I'd had the slightest spark of courage I'd have burnt the high school down at least.

At last, in the middle of November, I hit upon the plan of going over to the public library after I had eaten my lunch. Lots of other country students went there too. Most of them either giggled at magazines or hunted up art prints and photographs of classical sculpture on which they made obscene additions, or if more than usually clever, obscene comments. For over one happy week the Bully seemed to have lost me, for he did not appear at the library. Then I looked up from a dull book I was reading and there he was. He had my cap in his hand and would not give it back to me. How he had got hold of it I couldn't imagine. How I was to get it back from him, I couldn't imagine either. He must have given it back to me. I can't remember just how. Of course it wasn't the sort of hat anyone else wore, as you might expect. It was a toque, a red-and-white woollen one that Noreen used to wear. Every other boy at school wore a fedora or a least a helmet.

During the library period of my bullying he sat as close up against me as he could and whispered obscenities in my ear. After two weeks of this, being rather desperate, I did not go to the boys' cafeteria to eat my lunch but took my books and my lunch and went out into the streets. This was in early December and there was deep snow everywhere. I ran past the jail, down into the civic gardens, across the river, under a bridge, and down the other side of the river as fast as I could go. I had no idea where I was going to eat my lunch until I saw the town cemetery just ahead of me. It seemed fairly safe. I could eat my sandwiches under a tree and then keep warm by reading the inscriptions on gravestones and walking about.

The second day or the third, I discovered that the doors of the cemetery's mausoleum were open and that there were two benches inside where you can be buried in a marble pigeon-hole instead of the cold ground. To this place I came day after day, and I revelled in the morbid quiet of the place. I sat on one of the walnut benches and whispered irregular French verbs to myself or memorized the mineral resources of Turkey or the history of the Upper Canada Rebellion. All around and all above me dead citizens lay in their coffins, their rings flashing in the darkness, their fingernails grown long like white thin carrots, and the hair of the dead men grown out long and wild to their shoulders. No one ever disturbed me. People's fingernails and hair do keep on growing after they're dead, you know. Aunt Coraline read it in a book.

No one ever disturbed me at the mausoleum. The wind howled about that dismal place but no other voice howled. Only once I had some trouble in getting the heavy doors open when the factory whistles blew and it was time to start walking back to school. I usually arrived back at school at twenty minutes after one. But one day the wind weakened the sound of the whistles and I arrived at school just at half-past one. If it had been allowed, I might have run in the girls' door and not been late. But it was not allowed and since the boys' door was at the other end of the building, by the time I had run to it, I was quite late and had to stay after four.

Just before Christmas they had an At Home at the school. The emphasis in pronouncing At Home is usually on the *AT*. Everyone goes to the *AT* Home. The tickets are usually old tickets that weren't sold for last year's operetta, cut in half. Noreen forced me to take her because she wanted to see what an *AT* Home was like. She did not mind that I could not dance. She only wanted to sip at second hand what she supposed to be the delightful joys of higher education. We first went into the rooms where schoolwork was exhibited. Noreen kept expecting some of my work to be up and kept being disappointed. I was very nervous with a paintbrush so none of my drawings were up in the art display. At the writing exhibit none of my writing was up, I had failed to master the free-hand stroke, although away from the writing teacher I could draw beautiful writing that looked as if it had been done by the freest hand imaginable. At the geography exhibit not one of my charts of national resources had been pinned up. Noreen was heartbroken. I had learnt not to care. For instance, almost everyone's window-stick got into the manual training show. Mine didn't because I had planed it down until it was about a quarter of an inch thick, and as the manual training teacher pointed out, it couldn't have held up a feather. But I didn't care.

Noreen and I went into the girls' gymnasium where we saw a short, brown-coloured movie that showed Dutch gardeners clipping hedges into the shapes of geese and chickens, ducks and peacocks. The Dutch gardeners cut away with their shears so fast that the ducks and peacocks seemed fairly to leap out of the hedges at you. Noreen and I wondered how these gardeners were going to keep employed if they carved up things that fast. Then we went into the boys' gym where young men stripped almost naked and covered with gold paint pretended to be statues. After watching them for a while Noreen and I went up to the assembly hall where dancing was in progress and young girls hovered shyly at the edge of the floor. Some of these shy young girls were dressed in handmade evening gowns that seemed to be made out of very thin mosquito netting coated with icing sugar. Noreen had one of her employer's old dresses on. It was certainly an old dress, made about 1932 I guess, for it had a hunchback sack of cloth flying out of the middle of the back. Noreen, I know, thought she looked extremely distinctive. I only thought she looked extremely extraordinary.

And she did so want to dance. So we went up to the third floor and there Noreen tried to teach me how to dance in one lesson, but it was no use. She asked me to introduce her to some of my friends who danced. I had no friends but there was one boy who borrowed everything I owned almost daily. Here was a chance for him to repay me if he could dance. We soon captured him, but although Noreen clung tightly to him for a good deal of the evening and although we led him to the mouth of the assembly hall, all the time proclaiming quite loudly how nice it must be to dance, he didn't ask Noreen for a dance. So we went down into the basement to the domestic science room where punch was being served and thin cookies with silver beads in the middle of them. There was a great crowd of people in the domestic science room and before we knew it, he had given us the slip. Then Noreen said, 'Where do you eat your lunch? Kate was telling me how she makes it every night for you.'

I replied that I ate in the boys' cafeteria.

'Oh, what's that? Come on. Show me.'

'It's not very interesting,' I said.

'But show me it. Show me it,' Noreen insisted stubbornly.

'It's down here,' I said.

We went past the furnace room.

'That's the furnace room, Noreen. There's the girls' cafeteria. Here's the –'

It was dark inside the boys' cafeteria and I felt along the wall just beside the door for a light button. I could hear someone climbing in one of the windows. Someone who didn't want to buy a ticket, I supposed. Probably someone who came here regularly at noon and thought of leaving a window open for himself. Before I could tell her not to, Noreen had found the light switch ahead of me and turned it on. The person climbing in the window turned out to be my friend the Bully. Like a wild animal he stared for a second at us and then jumped back through the window.

'Well, who on earth was that?' asked Noreen.

'I don't know,' I said, trembling all over.

'Don't tremble like a leaf!' said Noreen scornfully. 'Why you look and act exactly like you'd seen a ghost. What was so frightening about him?'

'Nothing,' I said, leaning against the wall and putting my hand to my forehead. 'Nothing.'

The Christmas holidays were haunted for me by my fear of what would happen at school when I went back there after New Year's. But I never complained to my father or Aunt Coraline. They would have been only too glad to hear me say that I didn't want to go back. I must somehow stick it until the spring and the end of the first form at least. But I knew that before the spring came the Bully would track me down, and if I met him once again I knew it would be the end of me. I remember in those Christmas holidays that I went walking a lot with Kate over the fields that were dead white with snow. I wished then that we might always do that. I told Kate about my unhappiness at high school and it drew us closer together. If I had told Noreen she would only have called me a silly fool and made me hate her. But Kate was always more sympathetic towards me.

The first morning when I was back at school I found a note in my desk. All it said was this: *I want to see you eating where you should eat today, baby.* At noon I hid myself in the swarm of city students who were going home for lunch and arrived at the mausoleum by a round-about way. I couldn't get over the notion that someone was following me or watching me, which could easily have been true, since he had many friends.

I was just in the middle of eating my lunch. I was sitting on a bench in front of the Hon. Arthur P. Hingham's tomb. I saw the Bully trying to open the great doors to the mausoleum. But he couldn't seem to get them open. At last he did. All I can remember is seeing the advancing edge of the door for I toppled off the bench in a dead faint. By the time I came to it was half-past one so I started to walk home. My head ached violently as if someone had kicked it, which turned out to be the case, there being a red dent just below my left eye that turned blue after a few hours. On the way home that afternoon I had just reached a place in the road where you can see our house when I decided that I could not bear to go to high school any longer. So I went home and I told them that I had been expelled for walking in through the girls' door instead of the boys' door. They never doubted that this was true, so little did they know of high schools and their rules. Noreen doubted me, but by the time she heard about my being expelled it was too late to send me back. Aunt Coraline cried a bit over it all; my father told me the whole thing showed that I really belonged on the farm. Only Kate realized how much school had meant to me and how desperately I had tried to adapt myself to it.

That night as I lay in bed, while outside a cold strong river of wind roared about the house shaking everything and rattling the dishes in the cupboard downstairs, that night I dreamt three dreams. I have never been able to discover what they meant.

First I dreamt that Noreen was the Bully and that I caught her washing off her disguise in the water-trough in the yard. Then I dreamt I saw the Bully make love to Kate and she hugging and kissing him. The last dream I had was the longest of all. I dreamt that just before dawn I crept out of the house and went through the yard. And all the letters Noreen had ever made out of grain there while she was feeding the chickens had all sprouted up into green letters of grass and wheat. Someone touched me on the shoulder and said sadly, *I haven't got a spoon,* but I ran away without answering across the fields into the bush. There was a round pond there surrounded by a grove of young chokecherry trees. I pushed through these and came to the edge of the pond. There lay the Bully looking almost pitiful, his arms and legs bound with green ropes made out of nettles. He was drowned dead, half in the water and half out of it, but face up. And in the dim light of the dawn I knelt down and kissed him gently on the forehead.

The Ditch: Second Reading

A Geography Lesson

EVEN NEIGHBOURS on our street often ask me how I became a geographer, and my subject is so new at this university that the entire faculty council laughed when I was introduced as the instructor in a brand new course – Geography. Geology was already strongly established with an aggressive and well-populated department. You see it deals with the depths of the earth where the gold and the uranium are hiding to be turned into investment coupons. But my science is concerned with only the top ten feet or so of our Mother Geo and kames, eskers, moraines, ancient beaches of glacial lakes and disappearing rivers aren't very investable. So, when they ask me why I became an earth-writer and knower, I shyly and modestly say: 'Because my father dug a long ditch and I helped him.'

Only geography in its subdivision 'physiography' – the science of land forms – could explain the tragedy of my father's life. His farm happened to fit into the v-shaped wide ravine of an ancient glacial river valley, and so his neighbours found it, they being on till plain higher up on either side of him, oh so easy to pour their excess water down on his wheatfields and turn them into willow swamps.

So, one day my father suddenly started to dig a ditch right down the middle of his farm to let this neighbour's piss, as he called it, out of his land and into the municipal drain it should have been poured into the first place – south instead of west and east into his birthright.

If you were to look at our farm from a balloon, and you do when you examine the map I have provided for you on page

95, you can see that the long valley we lived in doesn't tip much, either to the north where it would then drain into the Little Thames, or to the south, where its excess fluids would hit the threadlike drains, ditches, and rills that eventually capillary into the Middle Thames.

The reason for this, I figure, is that fifty thousand years ago there had been a big glacier that gouged out a channel to the south, and then twenty thousand years ago there had been another that re-gouged sort of to the north. It's odd the way we talk about glaciers in our neck of the woods, but it's what we have instead of Hittites and pyramids and early archaic gods and Thotmes the Third. When I was younger and thinking of becoming a creative writing instructor, a course even more derided by faculty councils than geography, I once wrote a poem about a glacier slowly grinding down on a Eocene landscape with high mountains, biting the tops of these off – vague bodings of breast biting here by a giant icy lover? – and leaving them as granite erratics in the fields of our township whose visible rocks are usually Ordovician limestone. Translated into nontechnical jargon – this means that those knobs you see in Northern Ontario lost their tops to moving, shearing ice which then melted with them down in Southern Ontario depositing field stones in many a farmer's field. Barn foundations are made of them, well linings, and whole houses. The masons would ask you to haul your field stones into your barn yard, and then in the winter they'd light fires, boil water, and crack them open like pterodactyl eggs, then hew away till square.

I forget to mention that there were five acres of ground whose water didn't want to go either south or north and, after a brickmaker stirred up its ghosts, it became a permanent pond we call the 'clay hole'. Even Father never dreamed that THE DITCH would suck away its crayfishy depths; his successor in my mother's bed, however, did, with his engineering know-how, drill a hole through the southernmost field that nearly drained it dry until this great lover (me!) of catfish and crayfish took over and filled his smooth stepfather's insertion with stones and rushes. There's such a thing as carrying drainage too far.

So that now I own a wetland, a swamp, a marsh swarming with woodcocks, mudhens, deer (rather evanescent, invisible to the naked eye), rails, coots, ducks, the occasional mixed-up tundra swan, geese, mud turtles, painted and snapping – gosling-snapping, ugh! – mosquitoes, all of which, of course, helps keep everyone else's water table nice and high so their wells never go dry.

My father would not have quite approved, but then he made his living out of hay and wheat, not geography, and so he desired to force our farm's water (with clay hole exempted) to make up its mind – either go south or go north or shut up. The way south was blocked by an unfortunate knoll which broke him – a spade, our two spades could not bulldoze a way through something the size of the Step Pyramid, a fantasy thrown up by a particularly kittenish land-iceberg. Even when the water did get through the knoll and so away to Middle Thames – oh Shenandoah! – the fall is only two feet every mile. Sluggish are the ditches of our township until they touch the borders of Scottish-settled Zorra and then – deep declivity – rush, rush!

Never mind that, impelled by always being overgrown with too physical a body, I had a phase when I chose geography because I thought it was more manly than writing this kind of story. Times have been when I'd have given my teeth to be a scrawny ectomorph, but helping my father dig the ditch, alas, developed muscles, and as you shall see in the Third Reading, the final plunge to the bottom of the vertical culvert drain had to be preceded by swimming and diving lessons that, alas, broadened my chest. With the ideal of a heroic geographer, our professor also gave us a taste for black flies by providing an island in Hudson's Bay for a freshman camping expedition; professionally, I deliberately chose to help map the area just below Moosonee where my friend the glacier had made its Pleistocene last stand only fifteen thousand years ago. My virile blood sucked at by 1,000,000,000,000 no-see-ems as the locals call the black flies, I sloshed over tundra and muskeg, ending up no longer a MAN, but an imbecile as the discipline gave up ground mapping and, now, does it all from that moveable Tower of Babel – a satellite or a helicopter or an aeroplane. Or makes it up!

Still, I was not so imbecilic as to leave a profession, never mind how cowardy-custard about staying on the ground Ptolemy and Hakluyt found so useful, that gives me still bread and butter enough for one wife, and three little friends' support. I can't express how much I love them and delight in them even though there are moments when I could cheerfully kill all four of them, and when I'm sure they feel the same about their mad husband-father in one of his lunatic moods, e.g., when he suddenly ripped off all his clothing and dived into a creek we were picnicking by – no others present except a male friend, and I had forgotten my swim suit and it was hot.

When you eventually arrive at the final story in this trio – the Third Reading of the Ditch Saga as it were, you will find the difference between this account of my life with my father and how it really happened very much like the difference between the map of a jungle swamp and the act of walking through the actual subject of that map – muck under foot, no legend, clothes torn off by thorns, although in the end the 'real' jungle swamp is, in a way, a sort of map of itself, scale? – an inch to an inch and a mile to a mile!

The story then that I shall be telling in the Third Reading – an idea I garnered from my father's copy of *Gage's Third*

Reader which I read the first summer I could read. Digression: what *Gage's Third Reader* does is to break up long poems into sections separated from each other by prose and poetry of the shorter sort. For example, my father's favourite poem in the reader (outside it, it had to be Gray's 'Elegy in a Country Churchyard') was Lord Alfred Tennyson's 'For I'm to Be Queen of the May'; in the First Reading, she's pretty enough to have ambitions of answering a call to be crowned next spring; next you read 'The Heroic Serf' (he flings himself to the sleigh-pursuing wolves to save his owner's family from chomp chomp) and 'Abou Ben Adhem', may your tribe increase, and 'The Splendour Falls on Castle Walls', and 'How a Thermometer Works' &c. Now, two months later, you're ready for the Second Reading in which the would-be May Queen is prettier but – there's something a bit the matter with her lungs. Down comes the curtain, and the teacher has you studying 'They say we French won Ratisbon' or 'Blenheim', a really stunning poem in which little Peterkin runs to his grandfather with a skull and asks what it is, grampa, and receives the reply that there are lots of 'skulls' around the farm because the Duke of Marlborough won a great military victory here where thousands were slaughtered, thousands and thousands, and still no beneficial results visible. Puts you off war forever. And, at the end of the reader – the Third Reading in which, just like my father dying in the mental hospital unable to taste his final victory over his enemies, the girl dies the day before she is to be Queen of the May!

I'm sure it's not your favourite poem, but my father's choice of such a tear-jerker was coloured by the fact that he had a brilliant sister who died of eating cucumbers when she was twelve – appendicitis, attended medically too late – and she had been reciting the poem around the house before her appendix burst.

The story, then, which I'm telling near the end of this book, begins with father's death in the Ontario Mental Hospital near the end of 1934; and this hospital stands near the confluence of the North and South Thames rivers, and if you should examine a map of the area, our farm and us and the hospital are and were caught between these two rivers and its tug at weeping drains, and water flow, and freshets after heavy rains, and was so fated to be so caught since thousands of years before the caribou first dared to come to the tundra fourteen thousand years ago that then covered our farmstead and before the Palaeo-Woodland Indians came after the caribou to feed on them and clothe themselves with their skins and told the stories that slowly crystallized themselves into a civilization. In their stories there were two giant brothers – Sap and Frost who fought each other just like the North and South Thames for the water on our farm, and Sap Giant gave these ancient people chert knives and scrapers to process the caribou they killed which then they lost so that centuries later I would receive them as messages after long waiting in my father's ground.

As a boy, I longed to pick up, to find a magic arrow head or some such memento of prehistoric and medieval times on the place, but no luck. I think that the gods who manage my life hidden in my mind and my heart and my prostate decided that I should have to be first married and have the three tykes, but then it had to be before I first contaminated my magic walking world with learning to drive a car.

On impulse, as the taxi drove us out to the farm from the railway station, I told the cab driver to let us off at the front of the farm, so we could walk in the three-quarter-mile-long mile long lane.

But no, not down the lane did we walk. Crazy Father insisted we walk across a recently harrowed field.

I happened to look down about half a mile on, and there

THE DITCH: SECOND READING

sticking up was a flint message, an ancient knife – three thousand years old.

Since then, skin scrapers, elegant celts, round grinding stones, arrow heads have all magnetized us to find them especially wherever there is a slope down to where the great glacial river must have flowed, where the hunters would be camping waiting for the wild geese and the deer.

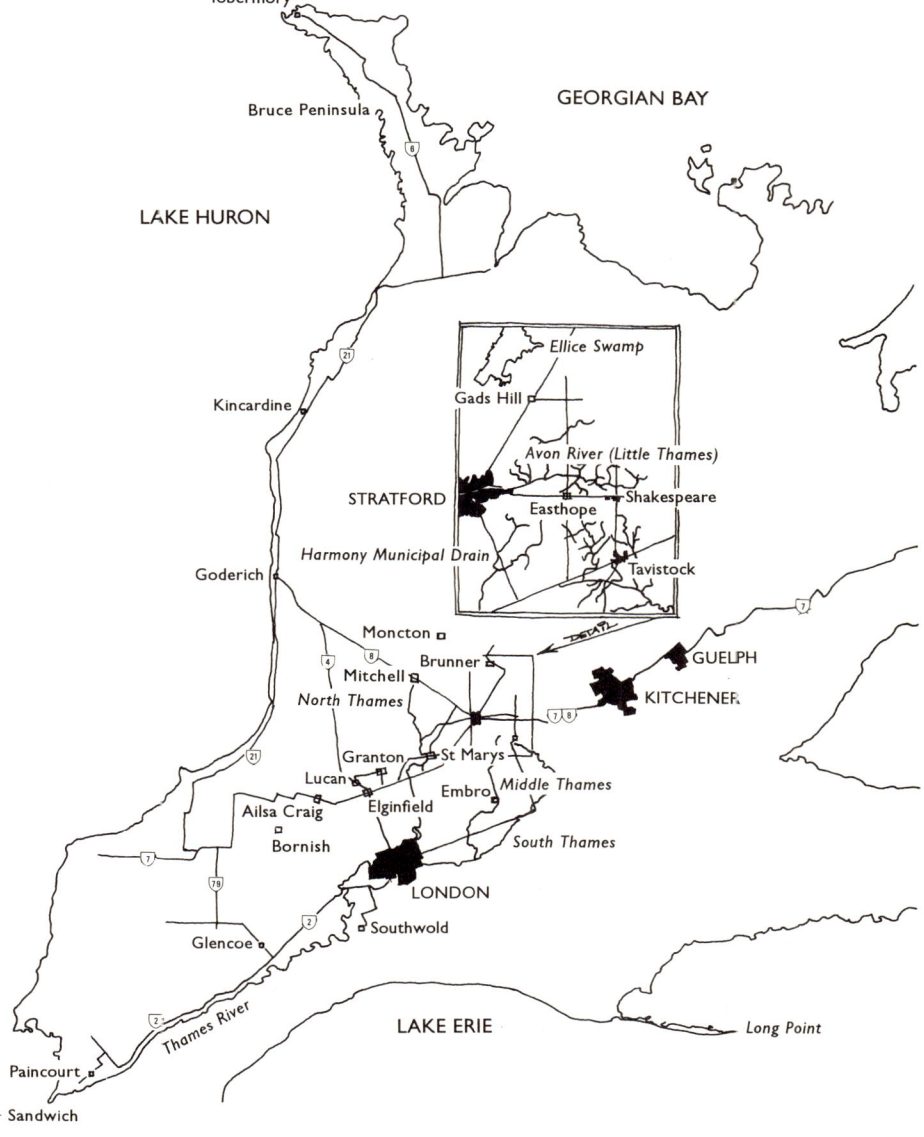

Master William Butterfield

YOU SEE, I'M THE ORPHAN, Billy isn't. Billy isn't the orphan at all though the way he's been acting you'd think he was. You'd think he'd never had no parents, no grandparents, no schooling, no civilizing influences anywhere near him since before he was born. You'd think he was an Indian boy who got lost and was being brought up by white people until he was old enough to find his tribe again. But enough just now about why Billy turned out so wild. I should have been the wild one is all I mean to say.

When I was three, my family completely blew up and disappeared. My father was a minister, lost like Anne's. He died and my mother she died with absolutely no relatives left behind to take care of me, so off I went to the orphanage or the Children's Shelter. By that time yellow wincey dresses were passé. There I stayed until I was about seven. As a place to stay I remember the orphanage had its points. Morning and afternoon we all used to be out digging tunnels in the yard. The yard was walled! Groundhog holes, tunnels, whatever you wanted to call them, that orphanage yard was just pitted with them and why the children started digging them and why it was such a custom round that orphanage, do not ask me. Why would we want to leave such a delightful refuge? In the orphanage there was a special room you were sent to if you were punished, really two special rooms both with bars on the windows. One room had a hard iron bed; the other a mattress of sorts, but I'm happy to say I was never in one of *those* rooms at the orphanage. Neither the hard nor the soft. Because I was very, not good exactly, but quiet and the sort of little girl who thinks a lot. If thinking could move mountains there would have been one in every room, only, when I was seven, a farmer and his wife decided to adopt me. The farmer and his wife had already had a child but as I looked so good and quiet they thought it wouldn't do any harm to have me too. Their own little girl had never come, or had died, I was never told. So out I went and hoped for the best. It's just as well. Mrs Stisted, the matron, flashing her many knuckle-sized diamond rings, was fond of beating up on anything or anybody who upset her: her assistant, Jessie McIntosh, left with a black eye and a lawsuit. Her daughter, Bella, separated from her husband, was punched on the mouth, and welts, bruises, and kick marks showed up on just about every body when Saturday night bathtime came along. Mind you, some of us asked for the punches.

Mr and Mrs Butterfield, they adopted me and sent in their hired man, Sam, they sent him in with a buggy to get me. When I left the orphanage, my there was quite a scene. I had a small valise, a relic of my mother's. Sam put that in the back of the buggy and lifted me up onto the seat. Alice, the girl who scrubbed, ran out from the back to kiss me and give me my present, a pen-wiper I have to this day, and I ducked down my head to avoid my friends looking at me. Sam climbed in beside me, the horse began to trot, I held onto the pen-wiper, and the orphanage, Alice, the children fell back away and back away behind me. The fresh bruise on Alice's cheek did not fade away quite so fast.

It was seven miles or so to the Butterfield farm, so the hired man told me when I asked. He struck me then as an old codger. He still is and hasn't changed much, but he never talks really unless you speak to him. At first on the way out I couldn't talk because I was thinking of the orphanage, how Alice, a big stout girl, had used to say that the thing about living on the farm would be the animals, that the animals both wild and tame, would be the thing about living on the farm.

MASTER WILLIAM BUTTERFIELD

So I had thought and as the buggy wheeled out into the country roads, so white in the sunlight of that day, I saw them come closer and closer to me; I really had set my heart on the animals that would be on the Butterfield farm, the animals I'd dreamed of, especially the smaller ones whom I longed to protect. I was prepared to search out and love, each in their separate haunt, groundhogs, weasels, mice, skunks, rats, muskrats, geese, hens, pigs, cows, horses, colts, all animals I'd just seen pictures of. There were a great many things I wanted to find out about them, because I'm greatly interested in anything that moves on four feet. At length I asked the hired man how many miles it was to the farm. He told me and I looked at him closely. He had the look of a favourite tough old dog whose job was to mind sheep or cows. It was really as nice with him as if a sheep dog had been sitting beside me, holding the lines and driving me out to the Butterfield farm. Sam had been the Butterfields' hired man for more than twenty-five years it turned out, and I asked him what it would be like at the Butterfields' farm.

Sam said, 'Yes, they did have a little boy larger than me. Bill was his name.'

Even then I saw that if I stayed, Sam and I would always be talking to each other, quietly; and I would always ask the question, then he would answer it. The once he initiated a conversation when I was as old as Alice, sixteen, proved crucial.

After Sam had answered my question, he was quiet again, and my mind filled up with a positive idea of all the things ahead of me; a room to myself, countless pets, a stove to sit by, and perhaps as much loneliness as I wanted. Even in those days I did not always want to be with people. The buggy whirled up and down hills, beneath oceans of green leaves transparent with sunlight, silver with wind; and the fields beside the road with the cows quite far away from their cowpaths and maple trees whose great high tops seemed, although it was three in the afternoon, still to be floating in the light of twelve o'clock noon itself. It was really the nicest hour of my life, then the fir-dark lane that leads to the house, then Mrs Butterfield lifting me up out of the buggy.

I am not really the person to criticize though I do watch things a lot, but I must say my welcome from Billy Butterfield was most strange. Mrs Butterfield lifted me out of the buggy, kissed me, set me down on the ground, and there was Billy. He was taller than me, with very blue eyes, very red cheeks, and really nice brown hair. I've never seen a pleasanter boy and I thought, well my heart always leaps up when I see a handsome person because I am just one of those people that fade into walls. So Mrs Butterfield said, Billy here is a sister for you, see. Act up nice now, Billy.

I smiled and reached out to touch Billy. He looked at me, and he cocked his head at me. The hired man led the horse away, and then Billy, not saying anything, stepped up and slapped me four or five times on both cheeks, laughing to beat the band all the time he was slapping me.

But I didn't cry. I just stepped out of range feeling terrible, because I thought he must have made some dreadful mistake, got his hands mixed up with his tongue thinking he'd been saying hello but really slapping me, – often you do it; and now Billy's ma would larrup him. But Mrs Butterfield didn't let on she'd noticed anything. She led us both into the house. Later on I met Billy's pa, Mr Butterfield, and whenever Billy went into his slapping act or otherwise did something strange, Mr Butterfield never let on either.

Since that time I first came out from town to the Butterfields' I've never left there, not even run away as most orphans do. Oh, they'll never get me to run away because it's right for me here at the Butterfields', and if the way Billy Butterfield has treated me has been a try at getting me to run away it hasn't succeeded. I must stay on. Now I have my own flock of Bantam hens, some of the horses quite affectionate with me, Mr and Mrs Butterfield like a pair of good old horses themselves. Sam the hired man like an old sheepdog as I said before, – I'm not going to run away from it all; it's too much. Billy can't make me run away no matter how he acts. Not with the nicest time of my life washing Mrs Butterfield's dishes at night and looking at where they are made on the back of them; then, after I wash the dishes at night, I always write up my weather diary.

So I guess since that first time he slapped me I've been slapped up to a hundred times. Billy and I have grown up together, he slapping all the way you might say. You got so as not to mind it. That's what Mrs Butterfield said to me once. After a while, after Billy had slapped you a couple of hundred times, your face sort of leathered up. It was no use, his Ma said, larruping Billy. He never cried, and he'd be into the slapping twice as hard afterwards. So they gave up larruping Billy, and just hoped he'd sometime, someday, stop doing it or wouldn't slap a school inspector or a bull with a bad temper.

Then I remember how Mrs Butterfield once looked at me after she'd been talking about her son Billy. She was standing by the water pail, she let the dipper fall back into the pail, she looked at me, – and I've just now realized what that look meant. Oh for years and years I've puzzled over what that look meant, turning it over and over in my mind just before I'd fall asleep. At first I thought it just meant, now I hope you'll be a good girl and not get into this dreadful slapping business. But now after the passing of years I see it was a look of fear at the queer slapping porcupine she'd produced of a boy. Then along with the look of fear and the look of hope there came really big glow of tenderness because even after a few hours it was easy to be seen I was a little girl who was quiet and loved watching things; someone whom Mrs Butterfield could easily love. You must get so tired of trying to love Billy. With me, perhaps consoled by my pet muskrat and the weather diary I keep, it's been easier.

So the first time Billy slapped me, I didn't let it get me down. I didn't even cry. Nothing was going to make me go back to the orphanage.

The second time Billy slapped me because I have quite a bit of spirit, I slapped him back. Billy looked hurt as if it had never entered his mind that people were apt to slap *you* if you slapped them. But in a little while I just let him slap me. Whenever Billy felt a bit low, you see, he'd slap somebody to cheer himself up. First Billy'd start to laugh; then he'd start to slap people. They say when he was little he used to climb up on chairs and cupboards just to get a chance to slap somebody, maybe an uncle or an aunt. Of course he never slapped his mother and father, but the hired man, me and his old Uncle Lorne and Aunt Peterina, we all came in for our share. As yet, when real company came, they didn't have to lock Billy up in the barn but it looked as if they'd have to someday soon because Mr Butterfield couldn't always keep leaping in between Billy and people.

After I got over my surprise at Billy a bit I just allowed for a few slaps and settled down to enjoying life there at the Butterfields'. Right at the very beginning I could see that it was turning out to be the real thing and the third year I was there they had my name officially changed to Butterfield. Now, I'm sorry they did this, but then, when I was ten years old, it seemed the last golden straw of a joyful load of straws, for at last I could give up thinking of myself as an orphan. All those first years it seemed I just used to march around looking at things I didn't dare to lean on, rooms in the house I didn't really feel it was my right to go into, places even on the farm. Then gradually I did feel more safe and sure, so all the people around me came closer in out of the haze and I saw them clear, particularly Billy. I was his sister now. Miss Mary

MASTER WILLIAM BUTTERFIELD

Butterfield was my name; Master Billy Butterfield was his. It never mattered to me then that that meant we could never marry. But the law is strict about this 'grass' incest.

One of the most typical things of him I can remember is when a relative of Mrs Butterfield's who was a missionary came to supper and would have stayed longer if it hadn't been for Billy. It was just no use bringing anything even as small as a Sunday school superintendent near Billy. It just seemed to make him lose his head.

Oh, you've heard nothing terrible about Billy until you've heard what he did to Mr Heinbuck though the windows he broke are pretty wild, the windows at the church too. Of all places Billy would play bounce-ball and ante-ante, over the church was one place, and one by one he broke almost every window. In the evenings he'd sneak off with his ball to play at the church, and you know he didn't just throw the ball *at* the windows. If I wanted to break a church window I'd heave a rock at 'em. No, he'd bounce the ball against the church wall and he'd bounce it till accidentally it'd go through the window he'd picked out to break that night. Why sometimes Billy would be a whole hour bouncing before he'd succeed in breaking a window and one night he bounced, bounced, bounced at the church wall with no luck whatsoever coming back all tired-out looking. Such a perverse boy he was, and our church such a nice tidy little church too. But after the dreadful fracas with Mr Heinbuck, which I'm not going to tell you about, it being too horrible, though funny too. Billy really had it in for churches; so it went on till there was only one intact window left in the church, so Mr Snelgrove, the caretaker of the church, *he* was gunning for Billy and whopped Billy black and blue one night, but still Billy would sneak over, but still Mr Snelgrove would catch him, larrup him, and one night the five Snelgrove girls, secretly instigated by goodness knows who, broke every window in their father's house from the inside and from the outside. Oh, Billy could persuade a person if he wanted to and old Snelgrove gnashed and gnashed his teeth, so I couldn't stand it any longer because I knew that he would really kill Billy this time so I went over very early one morning, it was fall and cold and I shivered, I went over to the church and broke the last church window with a stone. I could see why the thing was attractive. You feel exhilarated. In my case, I was also thinking of getting the misery over with.

'Billy Butterfield,' I said when I was fourteen. It was Christmas Day, after Christmas dinner, and we had come out walking in the snow, the snow blowing at quite a slant. We were just walking about in the snow, each with our Christmas oranges in our coat pockets. 'Billy,' I said, 'why do you hate people so?'

'I don't hate anybody,' said Billy.

'But you do,' I said.

Coming to the bridge over the creek, Billy suggested that we sit on the ice beneath the bridge and eat our oranges. I said I didn't think the ice was strong enough so I wouldn't go and Billy got very mad at me, said I'd never do anything he wanted me to, and slapped me. Then he said he'd run away because no one liked him, not his Ma, not his Pa. They all liked me instead. Why he'd walk right into town and ask to be taken in at the orphanage. There'd be people there who'd do what he wanted.

'All right,' I said. 'Let's go and sit down on the ice beneath the bridge even if it does break, and please, Billy don't talk about the orphanage. They'd put you in the hard punishment room right away with bars on the windows and all you can ever think of doing is to dig in the yard so please don't say you'd rather go there, Billy, or you'll break my heart.'

So down underneath the bridge we went. Down there the ice was crystal clear, very thick, and it all like a room we had all to ourselves shut off by the snowdrifts on either side. We sang and laughed, ate our oranges. Quite my nicest memory of Billy. Under the bridge, not a slap!

One Sunday afternoon in summer I heard him crying down in the orchard. He wouldn't say what he was crying for, but he just howled and howled like a dog who'd lost his master. Poor Billy, I wished I could understand him and help him.

Once Mrs Butterfield and me went away for a week on a trip and I sent Billy a letter addressed to Master William Butterfield. He sent me a letter back addressed to Miss Mary Butterfield. I found my letter up in his room just now. To think he kept it. The hired man is looking at the envelope now. We're both sitting in the kitchen. And Billy wasn't all hateful you know. There was something nice about him that reminded you of a very blue summer sky, something almost *too* jaunty like that you know.

Well, Billy learnt to plough and ploughed a figure eight in the meadow that wasn't supposed to be ploughed; he set fire to a cedar swamp; he let cows into things and horses out of things; but of course he'd always done that and some of the things he did *were* just forgetfulness, but oh, they did make you mad. Then he came home nine sheets to the wind, he'd taken to drink in other words, and all those Snelgrove girls – oh the neighbours are just gritting their teeth for what's to come, oh it makes me shiver. I mean the time Billy tap-danced on the drum at the Old Boys' reunion up at Mitchell and broke the drum starting a riot, that was bad enough. Yes, he tap-dances too. Now he's seventeen, just the age, and here I sit in the kitchen writing up my weather diary when yesterday Billy eloped with the second-oldest Snelgrove girl so that both her father and his oldest daughter (jilted!) are out after them and I think I know where Billy and Sarah are hiding out; down in the barn, as a matter of fact, so tonight I'll have to take them some food, poor dears. So here I am sitting with the hired man in the kitchen, and the thing that one shouldn't talk about keeps being not said. So I know sooner or later I will say it, so I'm almost ... all I'm remembering about Billy drives me to ask it.

I love Billy so much I wish I weren't his sister and yet look at what he's done with me having to watch all the years. I've been keeping my weather-diary through the cold, northeast winds, soft snowfalling, sleet today, January thaws, the hot weather continues, thunderstorm today. My brother, my brother, how can I protect you and I know half the time you've a perfect right to slap some of the people. They are fools but even if you slap and slap me, I'll kiss through all that till my love softens you. Right now I'm asking the old hired man what does he think will happen to Billy. My what a time it's been since that old sheepdog of a man drove me out to this place, almost ten years ago, and I love Billy but I've got to admit it. Sam is right when he says that ...

He says he doesn't know, but it looks as if someday somebody would just have to take a gun and shoot Billy. Shoot Master William Butterfield.

I thought so hard and deep about this that I couldn't hear the Massachusetts Sam Slick clock ticking away up above the jam cupboard in the kitchen and it's not a gentle tick tocker.

Then I cried, swearing for the first time in my life, 'No! By Jesus Christ no! Sam, he's the most interesting real man this neighbourhood ever produced! Is it Snelgrove going to shoot him? He couldn't hit a barn door at ten paces!'

'No, it's Heinbuck. Over the years he's been brooding and he's been saying the place to execute Master Billy Butterfield is in the forest when the deer season opens. Hunting accidents are hard to prosecute particularly when our inventive lad ties deer antlers to his head and makes a mockery of the hunters, also warning the deer, and letting muskrats out of traps and so on. I always feel it would have been a good idea to ration William's supply of Burgess Bedtime Stories when he was little. He's got allied with Peter Rabbit's view of things a shade too much.'

'You know, Sam, this is the most I've ever heard you talk in all the years since you brought me out here.'

'It is, isn't it. That's because I just made my will – into town to see lawyers, and it's loosed my tongue. You see I've left you all my savings and effects, Mary.'

'Aw, you didn't. Not your chewing tobacco!'

'Aw, I did, yes, and you want to know why?'

'Yes, I'm not worth it and besides Mother and Father look after me with an allowance, you know.'

'Mary, it was my idea for them to adopt you. I put them up to it. I heard there was a minister's girl at the orphanage – could your father's congregation not have done something more about you than to let you fall into that old Bible college fanatic's clutches, Ma Stisted? So I said, get her before somebody else does – with her you can be sure of her blood lines whereas those other little brats will burn the barn down first thing.'

I blushed furiously.

'But what defeated me was their changing your name. That means Billy can't marry you, and he does want to.'

'Then why the two Snelgrove girls up in the haymow?'

'Aw, that's a young fellow having fun. He's got to do something till he's wedded to you, given his temperament. I bet it comes streaking out of him before he's ever got it in.'

I blushed again, but overlooked the grossness of it, since after all I did want to marry Billy though it was the slaps more than the failure just mentioned that worried me.

'Sorry, I forgot I'm in mixed company – but I've been storing up all this for ages, and now I talk as a father to his son, or a mother to a daughter.'

'So, what next?'

'I asked the lawyer about how you get your old state of orphanhood back and they suggested that you run away and tell your mother, well foster mother, and foster father here – those two never-knew-what hit-ems, that you won't return until they get a deed-poll advertised that you're to be called Mary Watters again.'

'But where am I going to run away to, Sam?'

'To the orphanage. See if they'll let you in.'

I groaned at the prospect of meeting the Stisteds once more, but I could see that my friend, my real father and mother as a matter of fact (what is more thrilling than to hear about some unthought-of difficulties of love behaviour from someone who could only dare to tell it if they were related to you) had a good idea and soon I acquiesced. In half an hour, I was packed, the appropriate red and white lanterns were lit and hung on the buggy, and, leaving a note for the Butterfields who were over at the church hall playing King Pedro, we rattled into town and Sam knocked on the orphanage door which Bella opened with finger on her lips, since her chronically irate mother had just gone to bed and was a tiger when disturbed at such a moment.

❦ ❦ ❦

So I've been working in the orphanage for over a week now, and already I've collected a black eye, have scrubbed floors till my hands are red and sore, changed napkins on scores of incontinent infants, dried the tears of those languishing in either the hard or the soft punishment rooms with their barred windows, objects of terror and parental threats to every child in town. Perhaps the hardest cross to bear is not the mother's blundering sadism, but her daughter's tedious attempts to 'save' me for Jesus (she's a Bible college grad too), tedious too are her accounts of her off-again, on-again relationship with her 'husband' from whom she's finally gotten a child, one of the most difficult boys in the orphanage since, spoiled by his grandmother and allowed to assist her in her punishment routines.

'Sure,' I murmur to Bella – we bunk together in the attic – 'sure tell me about your wedding night.'

In the dark, I am trying desperately to write out my weather diary. When Mrs Stisted's light goes out, so does everyone else's. My minister's-daughter mask is slowly slipping and I can sense myself feeling blowsy and trollopy – just a shade, but Sam's conversation with me – particularly when I learnt the size of his savings, seems to have transformed me. 'Sure.' I'm not careful any more.

'Well, you have no experience of men, have you?'

'No, I'm not married like you, Bella.'

'After our marriage, a great big affair with me in white at the Ontario Street Baptist with Reverend Gonder officiating and showers and receptions and everything, comes the bus trip and our first night alone at the Sunset Hotel in Goderich. It was unknown territory to me, I can tell you, and to him as well. I'll leave out what actually happened – it always makes me cry.'

'Shucks,' I thought, 'the only part that might help me catch on about *it*, but maybe just as well if she's going to cry.'

'In the morning, I took the first train home to Mother and do you know what my first words were to her?'

Sleepily, I must have given the right reply, for: – 'Mother, you never told me it would be like that!'

When I woke up in the morning at some ungodly early hour, Bella was still sitting up telling me about her going back to him, the trips to see a doctor for advice, or so it seemed.

🌺 🌺 🌺

The children come flying in from digging their tunnels and say: 'Mary, Mary, green gravel, he wrote you a letter to turn round your head' – that's a skipping rhyme I've been teaching them – 'Your boyfriend's come to see you. What a swell!'

Black eye, apron, red hands and all, I follow them out the door and see a well-dressed young gentleman in a new blue serge suit just getting out of a familiar buggy to hitch up his horse to the sycamore tree that grows, and has grown for years, in front of the Stratford Children's Aid orphanage.

'Master Billy Butterfield,' I say.

'Miss Mary,' he pauses, 'Watters.'

'What in the name of the devil is going on here, Mary? The rules are – maidservants have no male visitors except on Sundays,' roars the orphanage matron close to my ear. 'Aren't you that crazy beggar that slaps people all the time?'

'I'm Butterfield Junior, but I have conquered that affliction, and, Mrs Stisted, I've come to take Mary away from this hell hole.'

'Oh, you have, have you? Got over your affliction? Let's see about that.' And she slapped him. The whole orphanage had gathered to watch.

'Don't think that will disturb me,' said Billy quietly. 'Didn't our Lord say that if a person smite you on one cheek, then turn and offer him the other?'

With a scream she hit him on the other cheek, and then slapped him for ten minutes until the children were crying 'Shame' and weeping, and my love's cheeks and face were covered in blood from her many rings which bit into his carefully shaven face, a handsome face shaven of its first beard for me. But, for my sake, I know he held out and, in the end, our Lord saw that she fell to the porch floor in a fit.

Her little charges cheered and sang at this.

The upshot was that Bella stayed, but her mother did not,

through severe ill health brought on by her failure to destroy my husband's self-control. The Children's Aid Society after many interviews and hearings selected me as the new matron with my husband as assistant, long overdue because of the problems the very big boys, some of them already men, had, even with hard room and soft room, being carted out to tough old farmers, always presented.

At long last, Billy made his peace with the church out at home – windows reglazed anew, Heinbuck, settlement out of court, Snelgrove, allowances for the two by-blows produced by his older daughters ... although my heart fell when nevertheless they managed to sneak them into my orphanage. How on earth did that happen?

My foster parents have adopted another daughter, Sam is retiring to live with us, Mrs Stisted is dying up in the attic, and perhaps the surest sign that the orphanage is being run on quite different principles is that the children no longer dig tunnels. How can they when the ground so used is now a croquet court and the rest of the yard a soccer field and baseball diamond with sand boxes, see-saws and pet premises?

At first, Billy was ashamed to be seen in broad daylight with his lynx-scratched face. When he kisses I can feel the ruts made by her diamonds embossing my face.

Our first little girl made up for the scars; she looks just like him, her countenance redeeming both our memories of the handsome 'dare-you' features we both took for granted.

After a while, little baby's habit of reaching up to my husband's face to touch the fascinating cicatrization scramble and squiggles did not bother him either.

Warrior, in the battle between flower and axe, wear your scars with pride.

The Ditch: Third Reading

'WHEN did you first notice that the neighbours were shutting gates on you?' asked the voice of a professional man whose figure I could just discern sitting by his fire while I lay stretched out on his parlour couch. He had a notebook, and my voice propelled his pencil across its pages, pausing after I did, recommencing when.... It was one of those Eversharp pencils I have always coveted since.

'Well, sir,' I replied, 'when I was sent over to help at Ally Porte's threshing.'

'Two years ago, or three perhaps? Rather young to be sent to a threshing, weren't you?'

Listen, I was just as overgrown as I am now – and I very much wanted to go. You see I was great chums with Victor McKersie, our hired man – he was going.

Yes, it was a barn threshing over at Ally Porte's, a lugubrious torture of dim forms coughing and sneezing away as they tossed sheaves down from the mows, sheaves which others below received on their forks and so into the threshing machine. Kids like me were emptying the grain that poured down a pipe into a tub on the granary floor, we emptied them into the big bins. There were three of us lifting and emptying away – one of us an epileptic named Orville. He came uninvited to all threshings in search of good things to eat; things to do were a necessary evil he sometimes avoided.

Abruptly, the grain stopped flowing down the pipe, for Mr Schmidt's tractor engine had broken down and he had to take off fast with McKersie to see if they could get a substitute part at a machine shop in town.

This left the whole threshing gang sitting out on the west

side of Porte's barn under the shade of some big elms, the men talking, the kids darting about on the big beams in the barn or sitting very still like myself in the long grass that Ally Porte's cows had, for some reason, perhaps sloth, not bothered to pasture as yet. No one knew I was there. Or surely, they would never have said some of the things they now were saying. About German women. My mother's mother had been from Hesse-Darmstadt, from a little place called Schiffelbach.

Some even crueller, younger men were bored with this, and, after teasing Orville, they locked him up inside the threshing machine.

Altogether, this threshing gang did not include first-class specimens from our neighbourhood. It was made up of: younger brothers, second-string hired men near the end of their days, aged bachelors, all purposely sent to a second-rate threshing for a second-rate grass bachelor (long parted company with a wife) seventy-five years of age. Slandering my mother and teasing Orville came naturally to this crowd; not one of them made a move to end Orville's affliction and they could hear his howlings perfectly well.

Be patient about my not ending his imprisonment, but you see it was more important that I hear what this other group was being told about my mother.

Well, the panel discussion on women of German descent started with the premise that, not only did they have yellow necks, a notion even Henry James is guilty of! but they came out to the fields in the middle of the afternoon and commanded their husbands to stop work and give it to them.

My first cousin, Jack, a fairly slow chap born on the farm just to the west of us, Aunt Vashti's boy, sometimes bad tempered, eighteen, spoke that my mother had come out to the hay field where my father, he, and our hired man, Victor McKersie, were working; she asked my dad to go off with her for a walk. Jack had then watched them go to the edge of the bush and lie down there. The lustful Kraut, she couldn't wait till bedtime for a 'gash' – a local slang expression of great ugliness for 'it'.

What Jack had not noticed was that Schmidt was back. So was McKersie who had been listening to his diatribe almost from inception.

'Whoa there,' said McKersie softly, 'why are you shaming your Aunt Jessie and your Uncle Jim, as well as your cousin Bert hidden in the long grass just behind you, shaming your relatives to this gang of has-beens. What business is it of yours that day what private business your aunt and uncle had between them?' Jack must have been blushing terribly in front because from where I was hidden I could see the back of his neck turning red! 'You foul-mouthed young fool, don't you know she came out with the medicine he has to take three times daily?'

Victor was handling this better than I ever could, so I slipped over to the threshing machine and begged Orville to stop howling so I could think about how to get him out. Was he in the winnowing box or the weed seed chamber or perhaps in the dangerous place where the sheaves had their strings cut by flashing knives?

'What's got into you, Jack?' yelled Victor.

'Nothing, you madman, you crazy son of a bitch, McKersie. Don't you boss me around, you're only a hired man.' Saying this, he slapped Victor who fell dramatically backwards dragging Jack down with him. Once on the ground, McKersie rolled over, placed Jack across his knee and smacked him on the buttocks about thirty times as if punishing a naughty child. Jack was terribly chagrined and laughed at, so he ran off, crying I think, swearing revenge, and did lurk about. The threshing went on without him.

Now, it was odd but when Jack's father a few months later

became bedridden, a strange thing happened to a tile drain they had both been digging not far away from our western line fence. Jack's father had been directing it to go south; his son made it turn left so its waters flowed under our line fence and down the slope towards our pond. Our farm is a long v-shaped ravine and it invites such manoeuvres which would not be impossible if properly asked for, permission given, and help also given us in handling the water. But this action of Jack's was unannounced and unadmitted.

The drainage wars had begun, and all because my mother's mother came from Hesse-Darmstadt!

Eventually, not only Jack on the west, but our neighbour on the left decided to drain all excess water into our farm and to let us take care of it.

It was on our eastern side that our most active and pernicious enemy appeared. Nameless he shall be, but nicknames are allowed, however, and we called him the Dinosaur since the tooth of a *Tyrannosaurus rex* had just been found in the swamp near Brunner in Ellice and the characters of both man and tyrannical, carnivorous lizard seemed very like. Others who had suffered from, before his marriage, his deflowering of their daughters, his sharp practice in driving bargains and foreclosing mortgages, they had other names for him; we found 'Dinosaur' fitted our view of the matter which was that of some innocent herbivorous but large *Triceratops* with three small protruding spurs on its tail, its only concession to the need for defence weapons in a wicked, predatory world.

Our family had always had trouble with the inhabitants of the farm to the east of ours. In 1884, an Irishman, a fence viewer of all things, named Quirk, waited till my grandfather went back to Ireland for a visit, and in a single day, moved a quarter of a mile of line fence over as close as he could get it to our lane, which hitherto had run down the centre of our front field. Since the fellow was a land kleptomaniac, and dangerous to cross, and, into the bargain, rather a favourite of my grandfather's, the latter simply gave in with these kind words of advice from neighbour Quirk: 'Shure, you can mover your western fence over into beside McCarthy's lakers in the swamper there.'

The Dinosaur, by way of contrast, started 'small' and experimentally; with an outlet possible but ten feet away into a township ditch by the Old Road, gleefully, at night, he instead dug a shallow surface channel over to our fence and let it piss water across our lane as that water slid down towards the aforementioned lake and swamp.

Next, spotting my father as often taking to his bed with melancholia, Dinosaur kept track of such events and, for every sickness my father had, he replied with another sluicing of water through the line fence all the way down to the second concession road – Hessestrasse or Pork Street, called so after all the meat the German settlers had in their smokehouses there as well as the place in Germany they had emigrated from.

Since he was violating, in the most Hitlerian way, my father's basic, primal property rights, Dinosaur seemed to be begging for a lawyer's letter; my father, however, could not summon up enough aggressive gristle to sic the lawyers onto him or even get our doitery old township fence viewer after him, in any case an Irishman related to Quirk and apt to have curious views about the inviolability of our frontiers ... Prone to sudden needs for complete rest on the kitchen couch, constipated, unable to move, with, in summer, a newspaper over his face to keep off the flies, not a swearer, good at wrestling, but totally inexperienced at fisticuffs, my father could only think of trying to block the invading water with his own bare hands rather than bring in the lawyers with their velvet gloves and verbal dynamite.

Armed with lanterns and old rags my parents and self

would sneak over at night to stuff the five or so drains of the Dinosaur shut; no permanent use, heavy rains soon flushed our plugs out.

One thing, I got to know our farm's drainage system very well. My grandfather had charted the whole picture on the back of an 1890 calendar, everything from the pioneer ones – mere lines of stones buried in the ground to hollow tree trunk ones to brick tile zigging this way and that, sending one set of puddles into McCarthy's Lake which eventually drains north into the Little Thames, and another set of puddles, less successfully, into a municipal drain the township had long ago, in an attempt at mercy, been persuaded to extend as far as the rise at the south end of our farm. These waters drained in that direction south to the Middle Thames. My first geography lessons were not just 'insula' and 'peninsula'; oh no, they were to imagine that twenty thousand years ago a raging glacial stream had flowed one way north and then, as the land sprang up from losing heavy ice, reversed itself, partly – south.

One day in 1934, I came home from school to watch my father digging like a horse in the centre of a field – he and mother had discovered another calendar map from the past which located a box drain, blocked no doubt, heading north to McCarthy's Lake. I ran for my small spade, a thin tillage specimen fitted to my physical development, and was rewarded by, at the bottom of a three foot pit, my first glimpse of some eels slithering away towards the north.

I think that in company with whole bands of overlanding snapping turtles, these eels came up the drain from the lake and from the Little Thames – to lay their eggs or whatever eels do. Of course, there was another set of turtles who went the other way to the Little Lakes and both sets of turtles were much run over by cars and trucks on His Majesty's Highway Number 7 & 8, the new Huron Road as opposed to the Old Huron Road previously mentioned – shortened to 'Old

Road'. Coming to and from high school, I was often late for both home and school because of my rescue attempts of these beasts until my parents pointed out that the only real solution was to camp out at the highway day and night while the migration was on – or pass my Junior Matriculation.

You may recall that earlier on in this story, Cousin Jack, at the threshing, called our hired man, Victor McKersie, a madman. Why would he do this, you may have asked, since my idol, our hired man, seemed to be behaving with logic and calm in defending my mother against the charge of nymphomania; well, there was another side to Victor that we at our house tried to ignore, for, because of certain things with pill boxes and 'dead' Huns suddenly pointing their revolvers at him, Victor occasionally mistook Cousin Jack for one of these clever Huns and, grabbing my father's squirrel rifle, would walk over to my aunt and uncle's farmhouse to shoot him. At the age of two, I am told, I and my dog of the day, Skippy, ran to meet him when, gun in hand, he came back from one of these raids. Aunt Vashti had, as usual, dissuaded him from shooting Jack just yet.

'Did you shoot him, Bickter?' I am said to have enquired.

Just when we needed McKersie to help us, the sheriff drove out to the farm one day and told the poor fellow that in three days he was to leave the county and never come back, or else.

Unbeknownst to us, he had taken a shot at Cousin Jack and missed; to his credit, that did stop water intrusion on our western borders, for Aunt Vashti for the first time found out what her son had been up to at nights with the ditching spade and post-hole auger. The attempt to set fire to the Dinosaur's barns was not so happy in its result, for Victor was caught with kerosene and matches, again muttering about 'Huns'.

Victor made as much out of his departure as possible. He had originally come to our farm with a grown-up's waggon, a bit larger than the waggon I had – *Sonny Boy* – but at one time much used by itinerant workers in transporting their trunks from railway station to employer's premises. So, he eluded my father's attempts to help him leave and, when my parents were away up town getting groceries and chicken feed, he had me help him down the back stairs with his trunk, still with his military number thereon, and then – haul it out to the porch where the waggon, the little waggon with its wheels recently greased, awaited a long journey up to Tobermory, the village near the end of the Bruce Peninsula where McKersie had originated, even having still in his portfolio an abandoned sheep farm, even having a girlfriend who still held a torch for him and wrote him pitiful letters which I had to read to him since he was illiterate. Next, at dictation, I wrote her a letter announcing his return and hinting at life for both of them on the sheep farm which I could just imagine littered with boulders, wild orchids and derelict house and sheds, nettles, raspberries, add some wild grapevines and lots of brush. The case was settled out of court with a conference between all concerned parties – the reeve, the minister, the warden of the county, a legion of veterans representative, the sheriff, the township constable, and the Dinosaur who made the fatal mistake of stating in front of the reeve, who had lost four sons in the war, that it was no use arguing Victor's military heroism and award, the battles he had fought in were senseless, idiotic, and of no account. Arguments advanced by the minister (of course, who else) that Prussian militarism had to be stopped were met by a rather glib retort that, said Dinosaur, *that* there high-falutin word you're using there, Rev, would never have been able to cross the Atlantic Ocean. I happen to agree with Dinosaur – if only they'd let the Kaiser go to his café in Paris, he probably would have, eventually, returned to Berlin without reviving Charlemagne's kingdom, but I am buffaloed by what you do when some strangers invade your place and you have a choice – run away to Cuba or put on white gloves and lead your men to certain death on the frontiers. With this Hitler, it's much more clear cut – we've got to stop him with our blood. But in the other Kaiser's war, we should have opted out.

So, what the community offered Dinosaur was McKersie's departure from the county. He never had returned home after the war. So strong was the bond with his regiment and my father that he just couldn't bear facing the world he had been brought up in – his parents, his fiancée, undirected labour, on your own. These parents had come down to see him at our place; so had she, but they had not been able to persuade him to return with them. One thing – he was terrified of the hero's welcome his local village would and did give him.

So, Dinosaur, threatened with publicity about his drainage malice, his disloyalty, and also a demonstration by the veterans – who had already so saved a fellow veteran from losing his farm – backed down from law although saying:

'It's not fair – just because he got a few medals and went nuts afterwards, he's entitled to burn my barn down.'

'Nor is it fair, neighbour,' retorted the reeve, 'that just because you went to Venezuela and made money hand over fist instead of to Flanders as my four boys did, that you should feel title to flooding out this boy's dad's land – shame on you.'

'That's not fair – why should he object to my draining my water across his land.'

There was a silence. Who can answer such insolence. I could –

'Without my father's permission?'

'Why, Bert,' he replied softly, 'you little firebug. I seen you there behind the vealing shed watching him light the matches.' The minister asked us all to join in a prayer for peace to be restored to the community. I kept my eyes open and could see my accuser striding back to his barn — we had met at the elms on our eastern line fence. His lie got under my skin.

The upshot of all this was that I cried so much at my going to miss Victor that he had me find my waggon and my equivalent to a trunk and my duds and pets and off we went to Tobermory – rather like the Bremen Town musicians, intent on fame and fortune and tinkling sheep bells.

Father and Mother caught up to us at Gadshill, an obscure hillock north of Stratford on Number 19, now paved, then only half paved down the east side. Extracting me from Victor's clutches, with more tears, they drove him and waggon and trunk to Gadshill Junction where, after their gift of a one-way ticket to Tobermory, he departed and – what a happy conclusion, happily married with three children, a thousand sheep, and an insane desire to visit us again and ruin his life the way Magwitch does by coming back from Australia in *Great Expectations.* We were too busy fighting the drainage wars to visit him, although we got to his wedding. Father was best man and I was a rather large flower boy.

Don't forget, that like Victor at fifteen when he joined up, I was still in short pants. There was a girl about my size also accompanied me up the aisle – similarly dressed in something too young for her, and out of our ceremonial contiguity and our mutual embarrassment at badly accentuated parts of our anatomy, grew penpal-ism and eventually worse.

In the battle of the drains, my father now played an ace he had up his sleeve since high school days – the city engineer in town had been a very close friend there when a student and now formed a sort of substitute for Victor. Since he became my stepfather eventually, I can't bring myself to name him, so I'll call him Engineer.

Since Stratford is built on a swamp, Engineer knew water inside out, and leapt at an invitation to take part in the preliminary investigations necessary before digging a beneficial ditch.

On his motor bike, a one-lunger with a panier, he, one Sunday afternoon, brought out a soil auger with which he violated, as he did later my mother's body – I'm getting like McKersie – the front wheat-field, slowly flooding and sending up dogwood and willow scrub. He wanted to find out what was going on in the subsoil regions. Well, his Orpheus returned with a Eurydice composed of three feet of big black snail shells, their type long extinct; once denizens of an Eocene landscape with a river rushing south. So, the moment my father began to dig the ditch, our hydraulic problems became an obsession with Engineer accompanied by a similar emotion with regard to my mother. It was Engineer who eventually toppled Brontosaurus Rex.

There had been a mercifully dry year, a year without winter, and in April, rising from the couch, tossing the newspaper away, my father seized two tile spades and a long-handled shovel, motioned me to follow, threw me a measuring chain; and to this very day I can still hear two subsequent sounds: (a) the sound of the whetstone sharpening our spades; (b) the rasping thud when my dad's spade sliced through the sedge grass and hit the planet.

Occasionally, I would come out to find him lying still on the ground, battling with paralysis of will; then I would take the long-handled shovel from his hands and work away. Digging the wet peat was rather like slicing through a big chocolate cake. Fun. Muscles.

As the spring turned into summer, we found ourselves opposite to our pond, a place dotted with prehistoric white cedar stumps, the spectators of my first lessons in swimming.

'Pearl Croft,' said my father, as we took our lunch break while a fresh west wind produced whitecaps on the pond, 'saved me from drowning just by that stump there in the middle, Bert. I had fallen into one of the old brickmaker's pits, crawled up the sides of it like a chimney till she was able to catch hold of me by the hair.' It was not your usual pond; years ago, Mayor Roberts of Stratford had a thriving brickyard on the east half of our farm with a huge clay pit which, however, he dug too deep and, like underground terrors, a disturbed and powerful spring shot up, drowning the blue clay and bankrupting his brick business. But not before the jail, the court house, the post office and hundreds of white brick houses had escaped the clutches of the water demons. Mayor Roberts wore gold wire earrings and bracelets – 'tis said, to keep away the rheumatism.

'How were things over at your grandfather's place yesterday, Bert?'

I told him that with my new diving abilities, sharpened by lessons up at the new Lions' Swimming Pool uptown, I had helped my uncles mend a leak in a dam they were building on their creek.

As we dug farther south, he informed me that when he was a boy of eight, he had won a mime contest at the Irish School. 'Mime!? –' a word I'd never even heard nor read about before, and certainly not one I expected to hear from my father's lips. He read his Bible on Sundays, and weekdays the biographies of political figures – Sir John A. Macdonald, Jan Smuts, King George V and such worthy types, but 'mime'?

'Oh yes, Bertie, we all had to imitate something or someone silently and I did such a good "milking a cow" that at a public meeting I was asked to repeat it, received first prize – a box of chocolates.'

The teacher was McGregor Easson, a star lacrosse player in his day, and I've combed old normal school texts trying to find the source of his inspired project, inspired for it nourished in my father a desire to run away with a vaudeville troupe. Every time Chaplin came to the Prince Albert

Theatre, he went in to compare notes. But – the singing and dancing stumped him. He was too shy to ask his parents for lessons. So, he settled for that most unmusical of occupations – farming.

At length, we passed the pond, actually it's locally known, even on old maps, as the 'clay hole.' And now we were at a spot where we met the remains of a ditch dug by my grandfather in an aborted attempt to drain the clay hole. At this place, I learnt that in 1905 when the Russo-Japanese War was in the news, my father and another youth had, with stones for cannonballs, and corked bottles afloat in grandfather's ditch for the ironclad warships, re-fought the Battle of the Tishishima Straits. My father, with his better marksmanship, had sunk all the other boy's Russian navy. Name of boy?

'Dinosaur.'

'He, play at toy naval battles?'

'Oh, he was quite a different fellow then. Not a mean bone in his body.'

'Well, what changed him?'

'Hunky-dory used to be his favourite expression. What changed him?' Pause. 'Going to Venezuela instead of staying home and joining up the way McKersie and I did.'

'Venezuela. Where'd he get the idea of going there?'

'Old Dinosaur, his dad, is some sort of atheist and pacifist – so he sent his boys down where they wouldn't get killed like the rest of us. I think his sons were overseers on a sugar cane plantation – I've seen pictures of them on horseback and – they could whip the lazy ones, and ... women. Power over – went to his head. Made him – the little tyrant of his fields.'

'But, Dad, it's not fair. You and Victor McKersie fought and suffered for your country, and what have you got for it? The sheriff tells McKersie to leave the county for good, and you have to dig this ditch because otherwise *his* water destroys your livelihood.'

'Robert,' my father replied gravely, reaching over the picnic things that mother had packed for us – to this day I can see the crumpled shells of the hard-boiled eggs we had just eaten with salt and pepper done up in screws of wax paper – 'Robert, why don't you know? Life is not supposed to be fair.'

'Yes, it is.'

'No, alas, no.'

'It's not fair,' I cried out, beginning to weep. Across the picnic things, for the first time, he reached out and put his arms around me trying to stop me from crying.

That afternoon, the soil we were digging began first to turn sandy, then loamy, and next to slope up.

We had reached the difficult part – to slice through the large hillock and connect up with the Mecca of the municipal drain. We needed help.

The next day, the weather changed, the sky grey, I found him fainted beside the stone boat we used now to transport our implements to greater distance. My father had dug as far as he could. I could not rouse him.

As I tugged him onto the stone boat and drove up to the house, I realized that he had dug – he'd dig ditches no more.

My mother was away at a Women's Institute junket, so I phoned the doctor. At seven o'clock, the young one with red hair came out. By that time, my father was up and about, but the news was – he must sign himself into the mental hospital at London for treatment as soon as possible.

Two days later, at the railway station, November, yellow sunset, I put my arms around him, my nose about level with his heart, and hugged him goodbye.

But in getting rid of McKersie and my father, Dinosaur had gone, had dug too deep and roused the wild spring of the Engineer, and I say 'wild spring' advisedly since three quarters of the force behind his demonic drive against the drain-villains issued from the sudden fire in his bachelor belly, a fire dumbly, but persistently, directed at my father's wife.

The first thing he did was investigate the new deed in which, for a dollar, my father sold the farm to my mother – a way of keeping the government from taking over the place to pay the hospital fees. In searching the old deeds, Engineer found out about the nineteenth-century aggression of Mr Quirk and so, he advised my mother to institute a lawsuit against Dinosaur for recovery of that part of the front field which Quirk, by moving the line fence over to our lane, had seized.

We won!

The neighbours, afraid of what Engineer might do next, began to talk to us, but Engineer counselled silence until he had brought them all to their knees. The neighbours had made the mistake of scoffing at the ditch, especially when the knoll stopped us, but with Engineer in command, we were fighting back not with spades and shovels, but with wit and strategy, and what large supplies Engineer had of those two mental implements. As he struggled with the problem of the ditch hitting the hillock, he went up country and bought two abandoned windmills – one an Aer Giant, like ours at the well, and one a Wind King. They were so happy, those windmills, to leave their derelict farms behind and have assigned to them the glorious job of sucking a wet spot dry and pumping it back on our neighbours' lands.

There was a great fuss in the farm papers of the day about your having a fire pond on your property so you could use the water to put out a fire – if you had a pump and a hose, of course.

Well, soon a well-built dam appeared east of the orchard across the slough to higher ground and – built for purposes of flooding the Dinosaur's barnyard? No, it was to provide us with water to put out grass fires in the orchard. Victor had once very nearly burnt down the driving shed if my mother and self had not pumped our heads off and rushed at him with pails and wet towels.

Engineer boarded with us now and proudly wore two hats – his job in town, and his job as unofficial hired man at our place. This caused scandalization in the neighbourhood that resulted in doors being slammed in my mother's face, and taunts at self in the schoolyard.

My father was well enough to come home, but my mother said no. He was not to come home. So he went out in the London district and took a job as hired man with a family called the Boughners. I visited him several times there. He didn't seem to mind his situation too much – that he who had once hired men was now a hired man himself. I thought he had numbed a bit though. As if my mother's betrayal of him hurt too deep to show, but was working away nevertheless. On the other – anything to get the farm dry again, I suppose. Give up your status. Give up your woman.

The spring of 1937 arrived with what at first looked like normalcy – people took out their cultivators and seed drills as soon as things dried up enough, but then – came a mighty change in the weather – a ten-day torrential rain, with an immense lake forming back of our dam, the dam that had supposedly been built to provide us with a source of water near the house and barns for pumping purposes if they started to burn down.

Well, the lake spread back into Dinosaur's yard and his middle fields just sown with grain. The water was seeking egress to the north – to the Little Thames. Our water had finally made up its mind! More rains came and the same thing was going to happen to us if we could not get the connection through the hillock working properly. Schmidt's steam digger had thumped away, dynamite had been used but just after the water appeared to be gurgling south at last, something happened to choke it up again. Iron rods were used to probe the depths of the culverts. My success in mending my uncles' dam was investigated and pondered.

Rubbed with Vaseline all over like a channel swimmer, and almost certain to die of either hypothermia or pneumonia, doctor in attendance, bonfire started to warm me up if I came back alive, uncles standing by, my mother, Engineer, and his workmen, for the third time I was lowered head first into the water seething in its vertical trap. This time I had a waterproof flashlight (Schmidt and Engineer had run into town for it) and sighting something dark and twiggy-rushy I let the light go on its string and lunged deeper than ever before. To this day, I'm deaf in one ear. I grabbed, inhaling water, and they pulled me up with a mother muskrat biting me and her young ones scrambling about their uplifted nest. Somehow a dry hall had formed in the culvert and invited trespass by beast. As I sank into a coma, I could hear people saying, 'That's done it, by Gee. Look at the flow. Good for the boy.'

After I got out of hospital, my muskrats and myself tested thoroughly for rabies, they telephoned over from London that my father's health situation had undertaken a change and that relatives should attend him. My mother said, that in view of the circumstances, that meant his son alone, and after being encased in blue serge with pocket handkerchief, still in short pants, I stood on the station platform watching her disappear to where she had parked the buggy, while fairy tale vistas of coal tip and distant fairyland horn (translate – train whistle of train from St Marys) enchanted me into a strange floating state. I had no idea that 'taken a change' was code for 'he was dying'; so for his entertainment I had brought over a new biography of Sir Robert Borden. But the moment, I saw his closed eyes, I knew differently. He still smiled when he heard my voice, and grimaced when some of the water I gave him dribbled onto his chin. But ...

Not knowing whether I should or not, I decided to tell him

selected bits of recent events: my embrace of the mother muskrat, nest and babies. He smiled. That the cataclysmic downpour of the next day had drowned his enemy and his farm. His eyes flew open. No smile of satisfaction though. Rather remembrance of happier days past.

'Billy,' he murmured, 'it said in the papers that the Jap navy came up in T formation, so you take that stick and push yours into a line.' Then his eyes closed.

Still, he did not die. I'm sure I kept him alive five minutes past his appointed hour with what I recklessly told him next. Then I faltered at something too terrible to tell even the dead, and when I faltered, the last breaths audible came.

I held his hand and bowed my head. A clergyman bustled in just as the breathings stopped.

An hour later, I was walking down the avenue of trees towards the highway, the village of Pottersburg, and the railway station. My train back left in half an hour.

The nurses had helped me long-distance the farm where my mother cried out, evidently fainting backwards from the phone. Engineer took over and advised me to catch the train back. Then, after saying he'd meet me at the Stratford station, he asked to talk to the superintendent.

I hadn't wept for my father yet, nor mourned. My feet slowed, I could tell because the trees stopped passing me in the twilight. I left the path.

The earth grabbed me. I felt grass, tufts of grass in my fists like somebody's hair. I cried out into the ground. Then I got up, went back to the path and two trees moved past me.

Again a stop. Again darkness and green cold hair in my hands, also against my bare knees, as I put my face into the earth's – that mysterious being my father had struggled with all those years now, finally, seemed the best comforter of all. This time I did not of myself get up; dimly, I was aware of someone powerfully swinging me up onto their shoulder like a sack of grain and carrying me into a sort of parlour where there was a couch from which I could see a tongue of fire darting back and forth from a hearth. There was a plate of food set on a table beside me which I couldn't eat.

Oh sir, let me go back a bit, and tell you more fully what I told my father – his enemy's fate in more detail:

'Dad, the wind swept the flood back into his yard. He was drowned – trying to save a prize animal of his.'

It was then that his eyes flew open and he was triggered to speak in the voice of himself as a boy telling his friend, as they played at naval battle with corked bottles in a ditch, to rearrange the Tsar's navy the right way. Then his eyes shut and I then said that when Dinosaur realized he was trapped on a crumbling pillar of mud, with open mouth and his sharp teeth he faced heavenward screaming: 'It's not fair!'

But pouring down on his bare head came the answer: 'It's not supposed to be fair.'

Now, have I not told you the story of a man, my father, tormented beyond belief by his neighbours' perfidy and evil toward himself and his wife, so much so, that one day, he took a whetstone and, while his son held up a digging instrument, began, swiftly and furiously and with secret purpose, to sharpen not a mere spade, but a sword – emblem of the complete overthrow of all his foes.

Sleigh without Bells
A Ghost Story
about the Last Two Weeks of the Donnellys

'ARE YOU SURE, Ephraim,' asked my father, 'that you know the Route well to your Cousin's farm?'

'Papa, I have drawn a map.' From my vest pocket I took the map I had drawn the night before with indelible carpenter's pencil which you have to put in your mouth to wet it so it will write dark enough.

The map was drawn on the back of one of our invoices for breeding services to mares and I saw my father's confusion as his eye hit 'Name of Stallion'; he does not read English and talks German in the bosom of his family.

My nerves can hardly take the delay I am so elated at the prospect of getting away from home for a whole week's visit to my cousin's place way down in Southwold Township through country I have never seen before. There is a flurry or two of snow falling and the wind whines a bit – all of which I desire Papa not to notice or I'll have to stay home and wait for better weather.

Finally, he turns over the invoice and starts working away at the map. Oh Heavens! he wants my indelible pencil – he is going to change my route on me.

My mother and sister come out with hot bricks and a jar of hot coffee and a basket filled with bread and cheese. Sausages which I hate. How I hate *all* the food – because I want to stop and eat at taverns; I have never been inside a tavern. I may even have to stay overnight at the Royal Hotel in Elginfield. There will be bartenders and chamber maids and hostlers and stable boys. My father gives me back my map. My bright visions fade, for he has drawn a different route passing by various relatives where I can stay quite free from bartenders and chamber maids. Dull, dull, dull. I know my relatives, inside out.

'Papa, this is a much longer route – I will be ten hours more on the road with two overnight stays – why?'

'Ephraim, for some unknown reason, the Route you have plotted out goes right through the Irish Settlement and right by "*das hasste Volk*" – the Donnellys. Don't you know they will steal your hot bricks and the bags of seed for Cousin Herman and your money belt and your sausages and cut out the tongues of your horses into the bargain. You could have chosen the Protestant part of that evil township, but oh no – right through the den of Papist Catholics you insist on going.'

'Who are the Donnellys? Why are they "*hasste Volk*", Papa?'

'Better I not tell you. Innocence craves communication with evil. Promise me that you will travel *my* way to your cousin's?'

'Oh yes, Papa.'

He kissed me on either cheek and hugged me; so did my sisters and mother – a custom I hate since the Canadians stare so at public demonstrations of affection. There is a last-minute checking by my brothers of sleigh bells, redistribution of bags of seed grain, inspection of the harness and bridles of the Clydesdales and then, with shouted goodbyes and wavings, I shake the lines and the horses pull forwards so that the sleigh bells ring – such a favourite sound of mine.

It is against the law, by the way, to drive a sleigh without bells – and also my father has provided me with lanterns in case of night travel, two red ones for the rear of the sleigh like a freight train, although that is not yet a legal requirement.

At Mitchell, it began to snow so thickly that my sleigh's tracks behind me disappeared almost as soon as they were made.

Five miles on, I came to the bridge I must cross if I were to take my father's carefully planned safe route. Just in time, I noticed that the bridge road was under water by about a foot. An earlier thaw had caused flooding and ice jams. I turned around as tightly as I could for fear of falling into the ditch and, consulting my map, made for another bridge six miles south.

A large hawk with two white circles under its wings flew up in my horses' faces and prevented us from crossing that bridge. Prevented us? Yes, repeatedly the fierce creature flew at the horses making them shy back and so I travelled down the tow path hoping for the best.

In the swamp bottom, I could see deer antlers. As soon as the wind carried them our sweaty smells, they waved their antlers and ran up over the next bridge frightening the horses yet again. I could barely control them and began to lose track of what township I was in, or county.

I was in the white tablecloth township of Snow and the county of Blizzard; magnetically, the horses were driving me. They seemed to know better than I did what route to take and by this time it was not my father's route, but simply one going south – the North Wind we had started with still at our backs.

At last there was a bridge and about five o'clock by my watch I saw another sleigh which I followed as darkness began to descend. At the tavern, I asked my location and they said I had arrived at Whalen's Corners.

Since they couldn't stable me, I asked their advice, and the taverner said with any luck I was half an hour away from Elginfield if I proceeded straight down the concession road to the chapel turning left at the London Road.

Soon I was out on my sleigh again, sliding past two rows of storey-and-a-half log houses whose doors I could just detect as being green. There was something foreign to me about the narrowness with which the farms must have been subdivided to bring the houses so close together. The fields about these houses and their log barns were dotted with stumps their owners had, after all these years, not had the energy to root up. And the dogs barked at us with genuine ill temper no doubt passed on to them by masters suspicious of strangers.

Usually at such moments of travel-fear in unknown parts, it is the duty of the sleigh bells to cheer you up – well, I could not hear them and, stopping to investigate, it appeared someone at the tavern had cut them off.

Yes, I remembered a surly, burly individual who muttered half-heard personal remarks about my blond hair and no Dutchmen being welcome in *this* township.

I could hear a cutter with very loud bells swiftly approaching down a side road and a great fear came over me, for did I not carry on my person a great sum of money which my cousin was owed and had I not heard stories of recent highway robbery south of us as well as a rash of toll gate thefts on the Proof Line Road leading into Antler River?

But the cutter turned in front of me to drive and disappear south.

Out of sight, I felt, it might have stopped to wait for me.

Was really dark now with the storm increasing its whirling chaos; a man waving a lantern in a very neat yard hallooed at me how much farther was I going?

I asked him how many miles it was to Elginfield or Southwold for that matter, my final destination, and he scoffed that both were far too far at all at all for such a cold and dangerous night, to turn in and he would put up both horses and myself.

He and his brothers took care of the horses for me while I knocked on the door of their parents' house which was instantly opened to me and myself made welcome without any questions.

There was a tall woman standing by the stove and a much shorter man sitting across from her. She was the tallest

SLEIGH WITHOUT BELLS

woman I had ever seen – six feet six, I reckon. There was also one young woman sewing, another baking.

They all came forward to help me unbutton my bearskin coat which my fingers were too frozen to do quickly. They were politely surprised at how far I had already come and at how far I would be going tomorrow morning. Should I not have chosen a better day? Oh no, I replied, the more adventurous the better.

The tall woman's niece, Bridget, was told to hurry up with the tea biscuits and the other girl, the seamstress, who, I later learnt, was Teresa Connors, was sent out to pump a pail of fresh water for my tea.

Since there was no one to introduce us, and they seemed shy of being so rude as to ask me who I was, shivering with cold, I told them that my name was Ephraim Flummerfelt from Logan Township up near Mitchell, rather closer to Moncton, perhaps, *um Gottes Willen*.

The wind roared across the room as Teresa entered from her pumping expedition, and so strongly did it blow that she literally could not get the door shut as the tall woman and the shorter man, both in their sixties, rose from where they were now sitting on either side of the stove as I asked them, apologizing for my rudeness, yes, but what were their names?

She said that she was Judith Donnelly and he said that he was James Donnelly. At last the door was shut; in the succeeding calm, I fell to the floor in a dead faint.

When I came to, Teresa was sprinkling snow on my face and the kettle on the stove was beginning to really whistle. Papist though she was, I thought Teresa the prettiest girl ever I seen and the sight of her afterwards sewing at some handkerchiefs edged in black made me desire union with her in a way I had never felt before for any other woman.

Slowly I rose and sat down on a chair which she drew near the stove for me.

'Have these fainting fits often, Mr Flummerfelt,' Mrs Donnelly asked, 'when introductions are going around?'

I was proffered a hot tea biscuit and a cup of strong tea which I used slowly to cover up my indecisiveness as to the best answer to this shaft.

'Mrs Donnelly, I'd been led to expect that you would be – different from – what you are to me now. I fully expected you and Mr Donnelly to have – horns on your heads and – hunks of raw flesh in your hands instead of – tea biscuits and cups of tea and – every sign of being normal, decent, courteous human beings.'

'Yes, I've no doubt there are many others, Mr Flummerfelt,' said her husband, 'who expect us to be devils.'

'We are,' said Mrs Donnelly, 'always referred to in the press as the Donnelly tribe, until my son, Michael, who's dead now, murdered, and in memory of whom Teresa is lining those handkerchiefs with black, he wrote in saying that we were not a tribe and that there were two sides to every story, didn't he, Mr Donnelly?'

'Oh yes, the trouble is, Mr Flummerfelt, there are worse than our sons in the township, but theirs is the larger gang, and so we are put to the wall.'

Just then, over the wind blowing, I heard footsteps on the roof and it seemed to me that the stove smoked as if some invisible force up there, besides the North Wind, were keeping it from rising.

I noted that everybody crossed themselves and looked rather uneasy until the shuffling sounds above our heads faded out.

'Excuse our superstitious ways,' said Mrs Donnelly, 'but since he died unconfessed, the ghost of Michael has taken to walking on our roof, sir, and occasionally warms his hands in the smoke of our chimney. He was waked here on the bed you will sleep upon tonight.'

After talking about the wedding party the Donnelly boys had gone to, at a neighbour's down the road, with the opinion frequently expressed that they would be dancing till dawn, the clock struck nine and it was bedtime, I to sleep with Mr Donnelly in a four-poster with curtains about it. Mrs Donnelly said she had bought it at the market down in London two years back since it brought to mind a bed in her parents' house in Tipperary years ago.

I slept on the outside of this rather unusual bed, Mr Donnelly on the inside against the wall so that to get up and do what people said he did that night without waking me was quite improbable.

Slept like a top, when just before dawn, I woke up and went to the kitchen door to obey a call of nature.

The storm had spent itself at midnight and I welcomed the red glow of the rising sun when I suddenly realized that I was looking in the wrong direction for dawn-glow; this was the reflection in the sky of a neighbour's barn burning down.

Almost that instant, before I had quite buttoned up my flies, the surly burly fellow at the tavern at Whalen's Corners appeared from nowhere with a man named Ryder claiming that – shouting,

'Where are the old barn-burners, old Donnelly and his missus? Come out, you old harridan and you old rapscallion, till we read the warrants for your arrest here.' Boldly, they pushed past me into the house.

'Why would I burn down your barns, Pat Ryder? Sure we've had no trouble between us for twenty-five years and no need for a fence even between us?' answered Mr Donnelly, getting on his clothes.

'Jim Donnelly, your missus said something about my son who was with the mob that came to your house last September looking for the stolen cow. That something she said leads me to believe – you burnt my barns.'

I pointed out, as did the girls in the house, that both Mr and Mrs Donnelly were too old to go out on a stormy night through high snowdrifts and burn down a barn; at this burly-surly, who turned out to be a constable, looked really put out that we could dare to testify that both the old man and the old woman had never left their premises all last night.

In his rage, Constable James Carroll, for that was his name, dropped one of the warrants so that, in picking it up, I had a chance to see that at first he had written the names of the Donnelly boys as suspects, but no doubt finding that their friends at the wedding dance would swear them an airtight alibi, *Himmel*, they were still dancing at the very moment we were arguing for their mother and father's freedom, he had then scratched out the names of the boys and penned in, with villainous blots and curious squiggles, the names of James Donnelly and Judith Donnelly.

Before I knew what to say or do, I saw this constable handcuff my host and hostess of the evening before and cart them away in a cutter, again with more than the usual amount of bell sounds, cart them away to be displayed as 'barn-burners' at a hearing in the township capital of Lucan in its council chambers that afternoon whither Teresa, Bridget, and myself were subpoenaed as witnesses.

Bail? Bail had been set by some high and mighty Justice of the Peace residing in the village of Granton for the unusual and unpayable sum of one thousand dollars!

Now, the two young men who had helped me the night before with my horses came back from the wedding dance and immediately asked me what had happened to their parents.

They did not seem surprised at anything I told them as if they were quite accustomed to sudden arrests although I was surprised at *their* theory as to who had burnt down the Ryder barns.

SLEIGH WITHOUT BELLS

It takes quite a while for a member of the placid society I had been born in up at Logan to get used to the fact that the burly-surly constable hated the Donnellys so much that he had probably set fire to the barns himself, perhaps with the assistance of Patrick Ryder's sons. It was then they learnt of the Donnelly sons all being at Keefe's for the wedding dance; again, too late they learnt that there were guests at the parents' house who could be heard as unbiased witnesses. But, by this time they had started the arrests of the older Donnellys, and it was too late to stop.

'Ah, they couldn't care less who burnt down Pat Ryder's barns,' said John Donnelly, one of the handsomest young men I have ever met, 'although Mr Ryder does, I am sure. My guess is they'll rebuild his barns for him to shut him up, and they'll advertise my parents as barn-burners because it drags them down and maybe we'll all get up and leave the township. Well, Mr Flummerfelt, we never shall leave! 'Tis a bit hard to think of my mother and father in the lock-up at Lucan though.'

'What is this you are offering me, John Donnelly,' I asked as he gave me a small twist of paper.

'Shake it, Ephraim,' he laughed.

'It's a bell inside there!'

'Yes, I noticed when we put your horses up last night that someone had made off with your bells, right?'

'Oh yes, after I left Whalen's Corners I noted that.'

'Well, it's very small, but ...?'

Later, I realized that he had found me a new complete set of bells, normal sized ones. Then the idea flashed into my mind that I had enough money, just exactly enough, to pay the bail of the Donnellys and asking the boys to help me hitch up, I was soon, with their blessing, speeding into Lucan down the concession road past some more green-doored houses all with their barking curs, and at the chapel aforementioned I turned right and was soon in the village of Lucan.

Right away I heard an uproar on the Main Street and I saw that Carroll was just entering the village now with his prey whose alleged crime of barn-burning he shouted about at the top of his lungs. There are several ways of getting into Lucan from the Donnellys' part of the township and we had evidently taken two different ways. Perhaps, too, Carroll and Ryder had digressed from the road for a while to pick up the deputy constable now set to watch the Donnellys with a drawn revolver.

At the lock-up, a great crowd had gathered – as they always did whenever the Donnellys were in trouble. Walking rapidly down the street, I saw at a distance Mrs Donnelly helped down from the cutter by a friend. Immediately she was recognizable – towering above all the other people. Both she and her husband were impeded by their being handcuffed, but their dignity and serenity were not in the least affected. As to dress, they had delayed things at the scene of their arrest while searching out properly ironed shirts and polished shoes so that they seemed rather like French aristos surrounded by unkempt jacquerie – Carroll's untidiness and unshavenness being particularly noticeable. Remember too that they were still in mourning for their son Michael, and so presented two reserved, sad, dignified people – one man, one woman – dressed all in black – even to their gloves. Black gloves.

A last question of bail was raised and I stepped forward and offered to pay the thousand dollars in gold. I was determined to delay my arrival at Southwold until I had seen affairs settled in Lucan, and through the good offices of the village postmaster, sent a telegram to my cousin to that effect. You see, I had fallen in love with the Donnellys, and I could not stand by and watch them disappear into a lock-up that, so ramshackle and unheated did it appear, would have disgraced a flock of hens.

Constable Carroll insisted on weighing my gold and the high-flying Justice of the Peace who had set the bail backed him up. I was interested in this J.P., a man almost as tall as Mrs Donnelly and of that cold, hard, Hibernian *Protestant* variety that when it seeks power, goes with its grey eyes for the jugular vein.

A jeweller's scales were brought and Troy weight much discussed and what a thousand dollars in gold should weigh. Alas, when my hoard was weighed, I was short several minims and grains.

'Hell weight, not Troy weight, is James Carroll's specialty,' muttered Mrs Donnelly to herself. All eyes were upon her, her husband, and myself to see how we would avoid this new wave of humiliation. Well, it suddenly occurred to me what had happened; one of the gold pieces in my father's strong box was badly tarnished and soiled. I had read somewhere that gold coins could be cleaned by passing them through your bowels, and so had, after supper on two nights previous, swallowed the dirty coin and never as yet passed it. Retiring to the lock-up's latrine, I soon returned with a bright clean coin, and Carroll reluctantly knocked off the handcuffs.

To celebrate, the Donnellys invited me to have dinner with them although it took a while to pick the right place because many of the Lucan hotels had been allegedly burnt down by their sons' faction during the stage coach feud. Or burnt by the rival stage line as well! We finally settled for the Western Hotel opposite the railway station.

'Mr and Mrs Donnelly, may, *um Gottes Willen*, may I ask you a few questions?' Mr Donnelly told me to ask away and I watched in fascination at how skilfully they handled fork and knife.

What I asked about was the strange absence of buggy or personal cart or even cutter at their farm. I imagined that their oldest son still alive, William, drove them about since he was a stallion groom like my father and would have to have some transportation, but I wanted to know more about this.

'Mr Flummerfelt,' replied Mr Donnelly, 'last September, we did have a fine double buggy which we and Bridget and John and Tom could all drive to mass in or to market, mill, or church as the saying goes. It was after one o'clock on a Sunday, when the Sabbath rules are relaxed so we were playing cards in the kitchen, and, say, a whirlwind blew up outside with black clouds and lighting flashes. We looked out into the yard and the double buggy or democrat or demicart was all outlined in a fearsome blue light – St Elmo's Fire, I believe they calls it, and – whoop! sure the lightning struck the cart and higgledy-piggledy – not a bone of its body or wheels be it iron or wood was to be found that wasn't smashed to smithereens, sir. All this with a fireball and an appalling thunderclap.'

Then Mrs Donnelly continued the story, for there was more happened; after nature's electricity, next the church's version of same:

'The next Sunday, sir, we walked to Mass hoping that someone would give us a ride on the way and a neighbour did. But when all was said and done, we wished we had saved our boot leather and stayed at home playing cards, for our new priest, that seems sent by the bishop to put us in our place, mentioned the double buggy in his sermon saying that God had sent a fireball to destroy the property of notorious sinners and that it was a sign from Heaven that good, decent people were, henceforth, to shun us. But there were parishioners of St Patrick's who were not yet afraid of Father Connolly and they gave us a ride home.'

'What about your sons – could they not have driven you to church, Mrs Donnelly?'

'William and Norah go over to Father Flannery in St Thomas, they are tired of being preached at from the altar.'

'It's just,' I added, 'that without a vehicle suppose you, one day, want to leave Biddulph Township?'

'Say, we are leaving in the summer after this fall wheat we have sown is harvested,' replied Mr Donnelly. 'My son James, who died two years ago here, bought us a farm at Bad Axe, Michigan.'

'I wish we hadn't sown the fall wheat,' said Mrs Donnelly quietly. There was a pause. I saw even in her brave eyes a flicker of dread. Then I said that I was surprised that they didn't have a bigger dog around the farm; everyone else had a wolfhound of sorts.

'For years we never had a dog. Then Detective Toohey gave us that little dog – such a pretty little terrier,' said Mrs Donnelly.

'Catches the rats in the barn – cleans them out,' said her husband, and they both rose to greet their lawyer, who, on appointment, had come to discuss their testimony at the hearing to be held later on that afternoon.

On their advice, I went to the Queen's Hotel and moved all my effects, horses and sleigh, over to the Western Hotel. The Queen's was run by the opposite faction and since my spectacular bail in gold that morning, it was not safe to stay at the enemy's hotel.

For the first time in my life, I felt alive. I suppose it is always like that when someone who is happy meets those who are determined to be unhappy. It was like a very quiet young person reading with relish the lurid violent events of a penny-dreadful story book costing only my presence ... well, and one thousand dollars in gold!

At two o'clock in the village hall, there was a huge crowd come to the first hearing of the incendiarism case against Mr and Mrs Donnelly. The three magistrates entered, two of them enemies of the Donnellys from many years back, and probably recently appointed for just such a scene as we were now witnessing. Mr and Mrs Donnelly answered to their names and pleaded not guilty, Patrick Ryder was called as a witness to the fact that his barns had been burnt down, but Constable Carroll asked for an adjournment to procure witnesses and Lawyer McDiarmid's objections were overruled two to one as was also his objection to a new ruling that neither Mrs nor Mr Donnelly must leave Biddulph. McDiarmid had asked for an extension of their bail and this was the condition. Again, our lawyer's objections were of nought. The court adjourned.

As defence witnesses, Teresa and myself were sitting by each other and I noticed that she had a very heavy bundle she was toting about; offering to help her, I learnt that she had a dressmaking job in St Marys, whither she was now entraining, and, my heart beating violently, I dared to offer my help all the way there by accompanying her to the station and buying myself a ticket to paradise – half an hour beside her ... on a train that went over such a rough grading we were thrown together more than once. On the way to St Marys, the train stopped at the Village of Granton where the adjourned hearing would be heard in a week's time.

While I waited in Stone Town St Marys for the next train back to Lucan (Teresa staying overnight at her customer's as she had at the Donnelly's), I happened to glance at the bulletin boards of the town's two rival papers. The *Argus* reported the hearing I had just attended and the barn-burning without comment – *the Journal* was anti-Donnelly in the extreme: 'Extirpate the Brutes – parents as bad as the children.'

'If a stone fell from Heaven,' I remembered Mr Donnelly saying, 'they'd say Donnelly done it.'

'And now,' said Mrs Donnelly as their farm hove into view, for, having returned from St Marys to pick them up, I was taking them home that evening.

'And now we should leave,' said Mrs Donnelly, 'but unlike

you, Mr Flummerfelt, when you continue your journey to Southwold, we cannot leave Biddulph.'

The trapped look on her face remained with me the next day as I sleighed south to my cousin's; the adjournment of the arson hearing at the Huron Hotel at Granton was not for another week, and I had time to deliver the seed grain and negotiate a note for the money I had used to bail out my friends. The thought occurred to me that I did not, perhaps, want the Donnellys to leave Biddulph until my gold was returned. Then, such was my infatuation with them, that I thought it money well lost if it meant their salvation.

My father's voice kept echoing '*hasste Volk*' and I know they have beautiful handwriting and dress well and the stallion the lame son William owns is the prettiest piece of horseflesh ever seen and their manners, but ... is there not a serpent underneath this flower? And yes, they did have friends, I met them, but – again why were there so few ones of their own religious persuasion? But it was like my love for Teresa; she could be a murderess convicted and sentenced, my body and soul knew otherwise.

One night, at my cousin's farmhouse I had a nightmare in which James Carroll and Teresa had a flyting match whose subject was – the Donnellys! The entire Donnelly family stood between them and every time Teresa spoke of them – they were my Donnellys as I have described above; but every time *he* recounted their alleged crimes, the most loathsome of which was cutting out the tongues of horses, they changed into snaggle-toothed monsters, the old man's eyes glaring with sadistic glee as he hammered the man at the logging bee over the head with a handspike; the old woman, like Lady Macbeth, urging her sons to each kill their man the way their darling father had.

But then, why did Teresa like them?

My father, who in the dream was scrubbing a red pig in

our tin bath tub, that we keep out in the woodshed for our weekly ablutions, placing it before the kitchen stove, scrub, scrub, – 'Ephraim. Ephraim. Scrub. Scrub. I have just found out, Teresa's father and mother run a bootlegging establishment in that village. They let a pair of young lovers sleep together in their spare bedroom when they eloped. They ...' scrub. But even in this spectacular nightmare, for me – I usually dream not about love even as most young men do, I gather, but my finding the pie cupboard unlocked in the cellar, I accepted Teresa's innocence even if she offered me illegal drink – it made no difference, I loved her, I loved them. At this point, myself now naked in the bath tub, my father began to brush me all over with a stiff wire brush, and I woke to find that my hand had grabbed my hairbrushes which I had set out on the nearby washstand. I was polishing underneath my night shirt with them!

There was a thaw now as St Bridget's Eve, and St Blaise's and Candlemas approached. I had to manoeuvre the sleigh to tilt up on the snowdrifts beside the road, and although as I journeyed farther north sleighing conditions improved, nevertheless, by the time I arrived at the Donnellys' concession road, in front of St Patrick's church on a Sunday morning, I wished I had brought some waggon wheels with me.

Tying the horses up in the schoolyard, I, in fear and trembling, tiptoed up the church steps and for the first time entered a Papist church.

Standing at the back by the holy water basin, I completely escaped notice because the priest was holding everybody spellbound with the following words:

'And no one is to give the Donnellys water for their horses. And no one is to give the Donnellys a ride in their buggy, or their cart or their waggon. And no one is to forget that last September, their buggy was standing outside their log shanty when a whirlwind and St Elmo's fire came thundering up to its divine destruction. And I say to you that whoever burnt down the barns of Patrick Ryder, their house – a ball of fire from Heaven shall fall on their house before this month is out. Kneel! All those who propose to completely obey this driving out ...'

Like thunder, most of the congregation knelt. You've no idea of the terror of hearing that rustling thunderous sound of all those knees hitting the floor, knee bones in homespun and worsted.

This kneeling exposed twelve or so who did not kneel, and one of these towering above everyone else, even the church's steeple, Mrs Donnelly and her husband who now left the church. I tried to attract their attention but their eyes were so fixed on some inner determination that they brushed by me to now stand on the church steps waiting. Waiting for what? As '*ite, missa est*' was said and hundreds streamed out to their carts and cutters, who could dare help them home?

I could not move or speak – transfixed with horror at the exclusion ceremony – and they had no vehicle to leave the churchyard for the personages that had brought them, the Darcys, would not give them a ride back.

Out came the priest, the altar boys helping him into his wolfskin coat, and he was approached by the schoolmaster at whose wedding the Donnelly boys danced a week ago when I arrived in Biddulph during the blizzard. He and his wife, his bride, he said to the priest:

'Father Connolly, Maria and myself were just saying how ridiculous these incendiary charges are against Mr and Mrs Donnelly. How could people their age be expected to run across fields of deep snow to set a fire and return?'

His wife added that the only reason Constable Carroll had arrested them was because he could not charge the boys.

To this the priest replied: 'No, because you played the tawdry, cheap little bride dancing all night so the barn had to be burnt down by the old people. Look at them standing there. They're no weaklings.'

The schoolmaster and his wife wished their priest good morning.

'Who do you think you are?' he shouted at Mr Panton.

'One of your parishioners, sir.'

'And a mere schoolmaster. Stick to your rod and your slate and your chalk and your abacus. Parish moral policy is my preserve. And, as for you, Mrs Panton, don't try the strong-minded woman bit with me. You see where that has got your tall friend over there. Alone on the steps of my church. Alone! Because no one at my bidding shall give them comfort or aid.'

Mrs Panton asked permission for them to leave and he dismissed them with a curt, 'What care I. Go!'

But now, my eye fell on the bride's father. Robert Keefe, who standing up in his waggon said:

'I, Robert Keefe, wish to tell the people, to tell you all as long as I have horses and waggons to my name, I shall always have room in my cart for James and Judith Donnelly to ride wherever they wish to go for as long – as long as ever!'

The priest replied by shaking his fist at Mr Keefe and walking swiftly over to his rectory. The Keefes, the Pantons, the Donnellys drove out of the churchyard.

Suddenly, it was night; it had started to snow again so the sleighing was easier, but I was somehow or other driving north, perhaps in the direction of home?

Yes, now, I know I stayed that night, that of February the second, with the Donnellys, but I cannot remember a thing until memory's magic glass has me leaving them at their door for my farewell to them as I journey to my father's home up in Perth County where my adventure with the: *'das hasste Volk'* had started.

John has hitched up my Clydesdales, brought them and the sleigh to his father's gate, I say goodbye, promising to visit them again and help them harvest the wheat that now lies under the snow in their fields. I can hardly hear their voices but Mrs Donnelly is begging me to take her to St Marys where she can catch a train to London, and transfer to St Thomas, and so finally see her daughter and grandchildren.

And so, leave Biddulph in which she is trapped. Nightmare takes over. She will hide under the buffalo robe until we are safe from the pursuit of her enemy, Constable James Carroll, but when will she ever be safe from his dragging her back to Biddulph? Has he not, I try to remember, not already dragged her back from St Thomas where she recently fled to say farewell to her daughter?

Mr Donnelly says, 'Yes, Mrs Donnelly, go with Mr Flummerfelt' – and my face feels increasingly warm, even hot, as if I were close to an immense fire – closing my eyelids tight, making me so warm that like the traveller in the fable I must soon take off my cloak even as I feel the cold snow blowing.

Imagine suddenly, loud bird song, summer light, an old woman in the ditch over there picking wild strawberries. There is an old man watching the old woman. He is shorter than she is. They are completely dressed in black even to their gloves. Is it my Donnellys? They turn away their faces, quickly...

Two gentlemen from the village walk into view – one, one of them in the special colour of his trade. I know I saw them that day I promenaded about Lucan for the first time.

As I hand Mrs Donnelly up into the sleigh, for some reason I stop doing that and she gets quite cross poking me in the ribs none too gently with an umbrella – an umbrella? I suppose you do see people carrying umbrellas against the snow. Then she says to me in a gruff voice:

'Good morning, young fellow, whoever you are.'

I open my eyes. Without warning, another time, although the same place, has crept up on me without bells, and – I look into the face of the Lawyer McDiarmid, poking me in the chest with a stick. I still think I'm helping Mrs Donnelly into the sleigh, but it is such a bright morning with white clouds and blue sky and a fresh breeze, not a freezing one. Over by the road in the ditch, I see, strangely, an old woman in black picking wild strawberries, her face averted as I look. I stand up without yet knowing what to say to McDiarmid. His companion, in special black that is code for something, I don't know what to say to him, or him ... Finally:

'Good morning, Mr McDiarmid. Mrs Donnelly and myself are going to the railway station at St Marys. Mrs Donnelly, we'll be late for the London train. Please get into the ...'

But my sleigh – it has changed into a waggon, the horses grazing unhitched in the grass of the Donnellys' orchard.

'You're not from these parts, lad. Where did you stay last night if I might ask?'

'With Mr and Mrs Donnelly. In their house. They very kindly took me in when it snowed so hard on January 14th. Oh, I was lost in the snowstorm coming south from Perth County. Mr McDiarmid, we met at their trial for incendiarism – burning down Patrick Ryder's barns.'

He stunned me with the icy water in my face of his reply that he, in his life, had never seen me before.

'Yes, sir, you have! You asked me to witness on Mr Donnelly's behalf before I made an errand to Southwold and once when I came back from there –' Here I looked bewilderingly around at the green leaves and grass. 'Why, yesterday.'

'Nonsense! Where did you sleep last night?'

'At the Donnellys' house – where else?' I looked round. The barns were there, very small narrow ones, but where was the house? There was no house! 'Where have they gone? Mrs Donnelly! Come back, please. Where are you?'

As he replied to this, I suddenly shocked at what appeared around me – four big stones where I was used to seeing the house – and I had lain in the centre of them – about where the four-poster bed had once been. Once been? Mr McDiarmid introduced me to Mr Mudie, the gentleman dressed in coded black and with a slightly overly smooth manner:

'Young man, get hold of yourself. You may be driven mad by what I have to tell you, so powerful and dangerous has been the illusion someone has cast upon you.' Sleigh bells for some reason jangled madly in my ears – a wrench of – a terrible black hearse sleigh bearing down on me. 'Young man, seven years ago, I received a box of burnt bones and tortured flesh already picked over by souvenir hunters.'

'Who are you, sir? I'm Ephraim Flummerfelt, *mein Gott*, from Perth County. My sleigh's turned into a waggon.'

'I am Undertaker Mudie of Lucan ...'

'Battered and smashed by a mob of vigilantes who broke into their house on the night of February 3, 1880, murdered and decapitated Tom, Bridget, their mother, their father. Burnt the house over their heads. Walked over to Whalen's Corners, called out Will Donnelly, got John Donnelly instead and shot him.'

When this young so innocent young fellow was told that, he cried out, ran over to each of the four stones, picked them up, kissed them, rolled about the site of his dream visit whose story started in the middle of that dream, did it? howled with grief. They were gone! Into the ground in a box after torment, fear, and hard fates. Then, Flummerfelt shouted:

'Then I did not help her escape. My Donnellys. My wonderful, lovely Donnellys. How could they have made so many hate you when – you weren't like that! I *know*. I met you. I want to die with them!' Saying this, he / I pulled out my case knife I use to cut the horses' and cows' hoof nails and pointed it to my belly, threw myself down upon it. But they caught me and prevented me. A wave of itchiness boiled all over me, then ...

The lawyer said that 'There, Ephraim, it is only a dream.' Only a dream – my sitting beside the girl in the train, the strong tea they gave me when I came in from the storm, the gold coin emerging from my body redeemed and new, Mrs Donnelly saying she was Mrs Donnelly? 'Many in these parts, like you, have seen them walking, in broad daylight, at twilight. Like Hamlet's father in the play, they died unshriven, and according to their faith, such cannot enter heaven or purgatory, or hell, but must wander the earth as ghosts.'

'Oh, Mr McDiarmid, it can't be a dream. They invited me out of the storm and the night and I can still taste the tea.'

Mr Mudie replied that generally speaking it was not wise to accept food from the shades of the departed. 'Occasionally, in a professional way, I am afflicted with a supernatural visitant at my undertaking parlour. Never do I accept food or gifts or even conversational gambits and sallies.'

'Look,' I replied inconsequentially, 'there's the impression of my body in the grass between the four stones.'

A young green man of bent grass dreaming of ...? No! Touching, tasting!

'Ah yes, those four stones were put there by the remaining family to mark where their parents' house once had been and the rental deeds to the property stipulate that cattle must never graze there – there are still fragments of the Donnellys there – their hearts were never found – shards of bone and sinew.'

'That's where I slept in the four-poster.'

'It is eerie – perhaps there is something supernatural about those stones, eh Mudie? They have made this young man dream in such a way I would have said, not knowing any better, that he knew the Donnellys and their house well.'

'Neighbours,' said Mr Mudie, 'when they bring in custom to me, and I grant that they have to be friends of the

Donnellys – the Vigilante families will have nothing to do with the undertaker who touched the dead victims of their hate. They go to the Protestant Haskett! At night, say these neighbours, suddenly the house is seen all ablaze with lights in windows and doorways, but run across to see it closer and – puff of smoke, *vanished*.' Saying this he took out a pair of scissors.

I asked him why I was being shown these scissors.

'Wherever you've been, sir, down among the restless dead, your nails and hair have been growing long.' 'Let Mr Mudie tonsure you,' advised McDiarmid. 'He's good at it.'

Do you know, I let him cut my fingernails and my hair which *were* longer, by my Saviour! Although, the thought occurred to me that I was already dead and was being prepared for burial.

'There are certain things we must tell you,' said McDiarmid when my manicure and cropping were over.

A customer of Mudie's had informed him that he had seen a traveller unhitch his waggon and set up housekeeping – inside the precincts of the four stones.

When Mudie had passed this on to the Donnellys' lawyer, he telegraphed Constable William Donnelly in Glencoe, at the extreme southern end of the county, to ask for procedural advice.

Constable Donnelly had told them that any trespasser on his parents' farm should be told to leave, but when Mudie and McDiarmid had come yesterday, I was asleep and looked so young and innocent and to be enjoying myself so much (I was probably on the train with Teresa then) that 'we threw an old blanket over you, told the neighbours to feed and water your horses, and – we'd wake you up today.'

I said, 'Which is?'

McDiarmid replied: 'You tell me.'

I said firmly: 'February 3rd, 1880.'

He replied: 'June 21st, 1887.'

'But it was so real! It couldn't have been a dream!'

Mudie allowed that if it were a real experience, then had I some memento of my visit?

'John Donnelly gave me some sleigh bells. One, a tiny one I kept back in my pocket.' I brought it out but its presence, its tinkling, lasted a few seconds, and then it faded away.

'Fairy bells melt like dewdrops in the sun.'

Then I thought of the handkerchief edged in black that Mrs Donnelly had given me in honour of my establishing their bail and out I pulled it. Suddenly the old woman and the old man picking wild strawberries appeared strongly and I continued: 'This was sewn in remembrance of Michael Donnelly's death. Look! There they are now. Picking wild strawberries. Look! Mr and Mrs Donnelly – they beg, they beckon me to accept some berries.'

At this McDiarmid said: 'Do not go over. Ghosts kill friends too, you know. Anything to have some company in dead land. They're lonely, the dead. So lonely.'

'We can't see the ghosts, by the way, Mr Flummerfelt, or can you, Mr McDiarmid?'

And with 'No, no,' Mr McDiarmid said that the handkerchief was a marvel. 'For it has Judith Donnelly's signature sewn upon it and should not exist because all the household linen was destroyed in the fire.' I saw him slide it into his pocket where it too has disappeared forever.

Against all their advice, I strode towards the ghosts and their offer of berries. They wanted my death so I could join them! But then they turned and looked at me. Their faces were skulls and they were laughing shrilly. They threw the berries at me and vanished. They did not want me! I was screaming – underneath the neat black bonnet and neat black hat, their skull scorched faces, teeth sharp.

And yet I wondered what life in their Will o' the Wisp and

Jack with the Lantern world might be like. Worse than. Hell! Came the annihilating thought. They had not been confessed before they died!

The two gentlemen walked me over to the waggon, helped me hitch up, and said goodbye as I drove out of the Donnellys' yard. I knew that my life would never be the same again.

They warned me that at the river, the ghosts might cause me trouble again.

At twilight, I came to a bridge somewhere in Blanshard, the next township to Biddulph. An owl announced its presence to a rising moon. From the waters of the river, four huge black gloved hands reached up and grabbed the hooves of my, the ankles of my horses who leapt up neighing in terror. We were not going to cross. We had come to the end of our lives. I would never see home again.

'Whoa, Wilhelmina! Quiet, Golden!' Teresa's form glided up from under the bridge. My heart fell – was she dead now too?

'Cross yourself, Ephraim Flummerfelt. It was myself sewed that handkerchief thinking of you and the power in you. Cross yourself.'

'No, Teresa. I'm not in the habit of...'

'Like this,' she crossed herself, then vanished just as I did cross myself for the very first time in my life.

Crossing myself, crossing the river, broke the spell I had been under.

The giant hands in their neat, black gloves slid back from the hooves and ankles of my horses and, instead of following them to where their owners wandered, we could go back to Logan township and my father Heinrick Flummerfelt's farm there.

James Reaney reads from the Erin 'stage',
Eden Mills, 1995.

JAMES REANEY is widely regarded as one of Canada's finest authors, a writer who is comfortable with a wide variety of literary forms. His very first book, *The Red Heart* (1949), won the Governor General's Award; he would receive this honour again in 1958 and 1962. From 1960 to 1971, Reaney edited the literary magazine *Alphabet*. Reaney is perhaps best known for his many successful plays which include the landmark trilogy *The Donnellys* and his popular books for young adults such as *The Boy with an R in His Hand* (1965), and *Take the Big Picture* (1986). He has also written the libretti for a trilogy of operas on themes from Canadian history. The first, *Serinette*, with music by Harry Somers, premiered in 1990 at Sharon Temple. Reaney's adaptation of *Alice Through the Looking-Glass* was originally commissioned by the Stratford Festival Foundation under the artistic directorship of David William. The play opened in 1994 at the Avon Theatre, and is slated to return to the stage in Stratford in the summer of 1996.